Still Me

also by Jeffrey John Eyamie

No Escape from Greatness

Still Me

A Golf Tragedy in Eighteen Parts

By Jeffrey John Eyamie

TURNSTONE PRESS

Still Me
copyright © Jeffrey John Eyamie 2020
Turnstone Press
Artspace Building
206-100 Arthur Street
Winnipeg, MB
R3B 1H3 Canada
www.TurnstonePress.com

Turnstone Press gratefully acknowledges the assistance of the Canada
Council for the Arts, the Manitoba Arts Council, the Government of
Canada through the Canada Book Fund, and the Province of Manitoba
through the Book Publishing Tax Credit and the Book Publisher
Marketing Assistance Program.

Cover image: Illustration 24318111 © Solarseven Dreamstime.com

Printed and bound by Friesens in Canada.

Library and Archives Canada Cataloguing in Publication

Title: Still me : a golf tragedy in eighteen parts / by Jeffrey John Eyamie.
Names: Eyamie, Jeffrey John, 1973- author.
Identifiers: Canadiana (print) 20200278991 | Canadiana (ebook)
    20200279017 | ISBN 9780888017130 (softcover) | ISBN 9780888017147
    (EPUB) | ISBN 9780888017154 (Kindle) | ISBN 9780888017161 (PDF)
Classification: LCC PS8609.Y34 S75 2020 | DDC C813/.6—dc23

MANITOBA ARTS COUNCIL
CONSEIL DES ARTS DU MANITOBA

Canada Council   Conseil des arts
for the Arts   du Canada

Funded by the Government of Canada
Financé par le gouvernement du Canada

Canadä

Manitoba

For Dan and Cam

Still Me

Prologue

THE BACKYARD
Manitoba: One Hole
Fallway Homes

Everything becomes impossibly still.

In this moment, time takes a breath and looks the other way, halting its goosestep toward the ultimate end. I open my heart up and draw my weapon back, the blade rising above my right shoulder. It's just me and this tiny orb.

The moment before I impart myself onto the ball is a moment I can only find in golf.

Golf is nothing like life. Unlike the world, my golf ball is completely at the mercy of my intention. I approach the tee box, settle, think think think think, waggle, make sure, look away, then look back, and finally begin my backswing, loading all of the force I can load into that club, all the while staring at the ball so my focus never waivers.

When I finally reach the apex of my backswing, and if I'm doing it right, everything stands still. I forget my hands. I forget what's happening in my chest. My whole world is a white, dimply sphere, and all the potential in the world is about to rain down on it, from my hands, arms, shoulders, back. Heart.

My intent is pure because it is at the height of its potential. It isn't real yet. This is still the perfect shot, perfectly still, not yet faulty because it hasn't been born. There's no memory here to haunt this moment. No pain. Not yet. There is only the perfection of presence and potential.

Golf is the only way I know to control time. It happens in the millisecond of that focused backswing, right before the violence of intention. It also happens in a four-hour round, at the bottom of an extra-large bucket of range balls, or during a short game practice session in my backyard. When I escape time, I escape memory. In that way, golf is an alchemy. A magick. I am a practicing magician. Not a salesman. A magician.

Everything becomes impossibly still. And then reality strikes.

My intent is made real upon this unmarked ball, which rises up quickly enough to avoid the practice net I was attempting to hit it into. It sails straight into the clouds and onto the roof of my garage, bounding off the shingles once and over the peak, from the back of the house to the front, before spinning straight down into the eavestrough. I can hear the polymer skin of the ball strike the aluminum with a sickly *ping*, followed by a wet *slurrk* as it nestles into some kind of gutter sludge.

Farts in a jar. I guess it's time to clean the conduits.

PRACTICE BALLS: 124 MISSED SHOTS: 79

This isn't a story about me.

It's not even a story about golf.

This is the story of my shirts. And maybe about life.

Faith and our teen boy, Payne, are gone who-knows-where, shopping I think, which is a good thing because if they saw me climbing a ladder to retrieve a couple (all right, eleven) golf balls out of the eavestrough, I'd never hear the end of it. But first I grab my aardvark-shaped golf ball retriever and clean up the backyard, stacking my not-lost balls in a pyramid. I put my practice net away in the Golf Zone of my garage and turn toward the mess of other fix-it-type bullshit.

I'm not going to lie. My garage looks like it's inhabited by the Odd Couple, even though it's almost exclusively my domain. The Golf Zone is organized with precision and forethought. I couldn't care less about power tools, duct tape, and caulk. It can live in a big pile. I need to wriggle the ladder free from the clutter to bring it outside.

I set the ladder up on the driveway at the front of the house. After checking for stability, I look down at my belly, the blue stripes of my Winnipeg Jets golf shirt curving over the round softness. I suck in a little, even though no one is around, like I'm trying to tell my gut to stay in place once I put it there. Ab muscles tend not to respond after fifty-some years of neglect.

I pat the flesh with some disappointment, look back up, and take a step on the ladder when it occurs to me that I'm going to get my shirt dirty if I go up there. And there's no way I'm exposing myself publicly, not after all the cajoling and mockery I hear from Payne about the horrors of middle-aged male toplessness, and how shirt removers of a certain age should require a license or permit.

I'll just be careful.

Up on the roof, I see that the eavestroughing is clogged with globs of leaves in varying stages of decay, and I need to go back to the Golf Zone to grab my extendable ball retriever. I make every effort to avoid contact with the guck-laden eavestrough as I come back down. Every effort.

As I head downstairs to place my now-soiled shirt and shorts directly into the washing machine, I notice the light inside my Hall of Fame is on. Dread overwhelms me.

Not to be confused with the Golf Zone, where my equipment lives, the Hall of Fame is where my memories live. It's a storage room for all of my greatest moments on the course. Maybe the not-so-great ones as well.

Nobody goes into the Hall of Fame but me. Someone violated my rule.

The Hall of Fame is the closet in the basement where I store my most prized golfing possessions. I've had the Hall of Fame, in some incarnation or another, for about thirty years now, starting with a cardboard box when Faith and I lived in a granny suite in Red Deer, then a vinyl garment bag when we bought our first house in Thunder Bay. Now we're back in our hometown, Winnipeg, with a suburban address and a custom floor plan, and the Hall of Fame has its own square footage. Sure, it's pretentious, but it's meant to be that way. Humorously pretentious.

Every time I go to a new golf course, I buy the shirt. In my line of work, we arrange rounds of golf with clients (or rounds of golf to get *away from* clients) about thirty times a year. Thirty times a year for thirty years. That's a lot of crests.

My Hall of Fame is like a walk-in closet of golf shirts—and towels too, from the times when I needed a towel, or if the club's crest was especially good. I have a wooden display cabinet that holds special golf balls, up high on the wall, perhaps where, if this was someone else's shrine, a crucifix or Buddha might be placed. I've got one of Chi-Chi's monogrammed golf balls in the display case, of course, and an empty space for a hole-in-one ball, should I ever get one of those. But the other balls are all keepers of one sort or another. Two eagle balls. A ball from my grandpa. Three monogrammed commemorative wedding balls, of which two marriages stand a fair chance of lasting. Lately, when I have time to myself, I like to come down here and just sit. I let the Hall of Fame suck me in, raining down memories of the great courses I've been so lucky to witness. Sometimes it's a golf course only a select few get to play too.

Once I started playing great courses, I became infatuated with golf course design. Canada is home to one of the best living golf course designers: Thomas McBroom. While golfers try to transfer their intentions onto a hardened glob of rubber and plastic, McBroom's intention is imparted on the Earth itself—the planet is his ball.

McBroom designs playable art, in the same way a Michelin-starred chef prepares their menu.

I've tried to get myself to as many McBroom courses as I can. I particularly cherish a McBroom crest on those shirts and towels in my closet.

For a solid half hour, thirty-rounds-times-thirty-years' worth of blissful golf memories will wash over me, and I can let go of whatever is happening outside of the Hall. I can be transported to the moments I associate with whatever crest I happen to see, from all courses, great and small. For thirty minutes, the focus isn't on James, the man. It's on James, the golfer. James, the salesman.

"Hello?" I call out, as though someone might be in the Hall, checking out my collection, or stealing it, perhaps.

I open the narrow door and slip into the Hall, not immediately seeing anything different. I've got the shirts organized by colour. It's a spectrum that goes from white to grey to taupe to blue, greens from forest to neon, and the oddball colours, from natural to cosmic. Hundreds of shirts.

I could have bought myself a car. A hot one.

Just as I'm about to turn off the light, something catches my eye. Rather, the absence of something: the logo is missing from my Victoria Beach Golf Club shirt.

No, I'm wrong.

Every single one of my shirts is missing its crest. On the sleeve or over the heart, all the crests are gone. Stolen.

I rifle through the hangers in disbelief, hoping it's only my imagination, or just a few shirts that fell victim to a very choosy moth, but no, all the crests have been excised from their place, amputated from the fabric, threads left dangling around the holes. Every single shirt is missing its identifying heart, like a memory ripped from its home, kidnapped. All my jewels, stolen. The McBroom courses too.

As I sort through the carnage, one thought keeps rising up in me: *she's finally had enough.*

I kneel and inspect the tie racks I use to hang my collection of towels—all the embroidery is sheared off. *After all these years, she's finally snapped.*

I should be furious with Faith. How could she do this to me? The destruction of the Hall of Fame should make me blind with rage, but it doesn't. Instead, all the stolen memories come flooding back as I cradle my broken shirts, my mangled mementoes. My house of worship vandalized, I sink into a reverie of golf like a shipwreck, slipping deep into the cotton-polyester murk. I pick up the gouged-out scraps of my beloved memories and try to stitch together what's left of them.

A Golf Tragedy in Eighteen Parts

1

MEMPHRÉMAGOG, 2008
Québec: Eighteen Holes
Thomas McBroom

I can't believe I am here. Outside the prosaic town of Magog in the Eastern Townships of Québec, there's a golf course whose privileges are extended to only a handful of regulars. The average country club is looking for hundreds of members. Memphrémagog caps out at fifty. It's a playground for the elite and the membership fees are about as much as my annual income, including commissions.

I'm a guest, my green fees covered by my employer, Boreal Building Products. I get brought in as an emergency fourth player because the CEO, Karl, has decided his gout is too painful to let him walk the course. I also happened to be at the same sales meeting in Montreal the day before with one of our crown jewel home supply clients, which probably helps my case.

From the clubhouse, which looks like an eighteenth-century English manor, I can see Lake Memphrémagog through a clearing in the trees to the right. Bob Ross couldn't paint a lake any more picturesque. The golf course lies beneath me and all around, like I'm being offered a preview from the clubhouse of the experience to come. It's an inspired design, and I'm of the age where my curiosity about the design of things is beginning to blossom.

As I marvel at my carefully manicured surroundings, only two hours' drive from Montreal, I think about the designer, Thomas McBroom, Canada's greatest living golf course architect. A human being did this. A person created this sequence; carved it right out of the landscape to turn nature into a test. I'm not sure if I believe that there's an unseen, all-powerful bearded guy sitting in the clouds, testing my morality at every turn, but I am certain that McBroom has designed this course to test me.

On this day, as a fairly green sales manager, I get the feeling I'm punching way above my weight class here. It's not just the exclusive, challenging course. It's the golfers. Golfers who are about to teach me the meaning of the term "FISM."

Gene, the CEO of one of North America's largest building supply distributors, will be my teacher. Joining us are two of his VPs: Vance, the VP of marketing, and Gordon in acquisitions, but I can't recall who is who. They could be Gene's twin sons, except sons would never kowtow and genuflect every time their father looked at them.

Selling product is not why I'm here. In terms of a sale, the decision has been made already. The CEOs know each other. They do CEO activities together, like golf at one-percenter courses and fly their private jets around in circles. It's not like I need to convince Gene to buy from us. It's a question of how much. My mission is to golf like I know what I'm doing and make CEO Gene smile with me but not laugh at me. I need to play the round and get out of here without bringing shame upon my employers, like a Japanese salaryman trying to avoid *haji*.

The commission from a sale of this magnitude would make my year. What's more, if I impress Gene, I might be able to pump up the numbers on his purchase order, so I'm doing my best James-the-Salesman act: personable, PG-rated, pleasant. A commission like this could pay for Payne's Montessori tuition, and Faith tells me that's what he needs. I have a lot of reasons to play my best golf, to be cordial but quiet while basking in the splendour of this expression of golf unlike anything I've ever experienced.

Plenty of reason not to be me.

There are no power carts at Memphrémagog. Walking only. The course is in such pristine condition that it looks like it has never been played before. Mist rises from the earth, tinged with a golden hue from the morning rays of a June sun. The theme song for the Masters tournament plays in my head; that lilting piano lullaby they play every spring at Augusta National. That tune oozes privilege and exclusivity and nostalgia. Memphrémagog conjures up those vernal notes for me.

I learn quickly that the greens here are not to be trifled with. They are undulating and lightning-quick. I know they measure green speed using a Stimpmeter, so I tell the guy I think is Vance that this green must be a lot of stimps.

Honestly, I have no idea whether two or two hundred is a lot of stimps. I probably should have looked it up. Vance grins back at me, murmurs something inaudible that has the cadence of a quippy reply, so I say "yeah" and chortle.

The first tee gives a downhill view of a dogleg right. A bunker sets up in the exact location you want to put the ball, in the crook of the elbow. I can't see the green from the tees.

Gene has the honour of the first shot, because he's Gene. He's a thick, bullmastiff of a man, bow-legged and potbellied and unabashedly a CEO of a major national corporation. An alpha from those old days when men thought it was good to act like an intimidating, mindless dog. It got Gene this far. He doesn't need to change, even if the world has.

His form is typical of an out-of-shape old man who golfs a lot: short swing, no twist to it. Simply one violent strike with a quick follow-through and, of course, Gene's drive lands in perfect position.

I don't know if there's such a thing as divine justice, but I do know that fortune is not divided equally among us humans. I know the reason why Gene's shitty technique lands him a perfect drive; it's the same reason he's the CEO of a major national home supply corporation. It's because he's Gene.

Vance is younger and stronger, but he sits his ball on the tee so ridiculously high that I suspect he has skyed this drive on purpose, so as not to show Gene up. Vance's opening shot lofts high and short and left, rolling over a hump and skittering off into the leftward rough. It's a longer shot than Gene's. Vance looks embarrassed.

Gordon does right by his career aspirations and fires his ball off the hosel of the club—the curvy part where the head becomes shaft—making his shot squib into the ground at an earth-hugging diagonal. The spin snakes his shot into a thick patch of rough about a hundred yards away.

My turn. With tee in hand, I stride to the box and survey the hole, all the while channelling an alter ego I've been grooming to take care of moments like this. James the Golfer isn't me; he doesn't get nervous when strangers watch him try to perform. Likewise, James the Salesman is so funny. He really gets you. He can give you what you need. James the Salesman isn't really me, either. But this combination of two men who aren't me is what I'm trying to channel right now so I can get this ball down the track to get along with the rest of my foursome and not blow the sale.

Golfing with less-than-full authenticity doesn't pay off. I swing the driver like it's a baseball bat and barely skim the top of the ball off the tee, placing so much topspin on it that it bounces into the turf of the tee box and bounds forward, perhaps fifty yards.

What do I do? Take a mulligan with guys I've never met before on the very first hole? Gordon motions toward me, indicating it's his turn, but Gene holds up a hand and says, "Ah-ah-ahhh. Looks like a FISM." Gordon halts.

I have no idea what Gene is saying, but I know that I'm farthest from the flag and there's no mulligan in my future, so I hustle up to my ball, embarrassed at how milquetoast it was. I quietly eke out a triple-bogey seven, every shot different than the last. Being consistently bad would score better than being this inconsistent. Meanwhile, Gene makes par look easy and the yes-men each make a double.

"You got kids?" Gene asks me as we walk off the first and head for the par-5 second.

"A five-year-old boy." This is the third day of my trip and it doesn't feel like an escape anymore. I'm thinking about Faith and Payne increasingly more, despite my best efforts. So I run the list of justifications through my head:

You're bringing home the bacon.

You're better in small doses.

You don't have the stamina to be at home for that long anyway.

This is the way these business trips always go. By day four, I'm ready to go back home. And then by day four at home, I'm ready to hit a course.

"That's what life's about," Gene says. "Or so they tell me."

"No kids?"

Gene makes a face like he tastes something bitter. "Not for me".

Gene pauses to inject his tee into the earth, then says, "I decided to build something bigger."

I have no choice but to nod. I know he's referring to the business he runs, and sure, business is a big deal, but it doesn't take a genius to figure out you need to share and pass it on. Even I can figure it out.

It's five hundred and sixty yards to the centre of the elevated green from the blue tees on this par-5, and despite its relative straightness, the hole is treacherous majesty. Again, of the four of us, I hit the shortest, and I can see Gene is bemused, and so are his execu-clones.

In golf, when you're away—farthest from the flag—you go next. There's an exception, on courses that are trying to churn through as many players as possible, called "ready golf." When you're ready, and the away player isn't ready, you play. At Memphrémagog, there's no rush. It's all formality here.

Gene gets tired of waiting for me and plays ready golf.

An alarm sounds in my head. I'm blowing it. "Sorry," I call out to the others as I hurry it up. Finally, my sixth shot lands on the green, just trickling past the fringe and onto the putting surface.

I'm still away.

As I make the eternal walk from my bag to my ball, putter in hand, I can sense the three of them examining me. Since I didn't expect to be a part of this game, the only golf shirt I had in my suitcase was an old one from Victoria Beach. I was hoping to play some golf on this business trip, but I didn't anticipate anything this elite. Suddenly I wish I was duffing my way down a municipal course somewhere else.

The green is long and egg-shaped once you elude the narrow strip of approaching fairway bookended by two inkblot-shaped bunkers; I'm probably thirty feet from the pin and I can't figure out how many different breaks there are. Two? Three? It seems to go mostly uphill, but not entirely.

I strike the ball far too lightly. The other guys are not twelve feet from the hole. My ball goes left, then right, stopping twenty feet away.

"FISM once again," Gene says, and the yes-men chuckle with him.

Too aggravated to care, I march to my ball, draw my putter back like a broken pendulum, and let it fly. I smash the ball past the cup, between two other golf balls, leaving it farthest away once again.

"What did you say your name was?" Gene says, and the question makes the bottom of my stomach drop.

"Jim Khoury," I say through gritted teeth, trying to contain my sense of *haji*. He wants my name so he can report me to Karl and get me shit-canned.

"Jim Khoury is the grand champion of FISM, eh boys?" Guffaws at my expense.

The words erupt out of me: "Okay, FISM. Why don't you tell me what the hell a 'FISM' is?"

"He doesn't know what FISM is," Vance tells Gordon, or vice versa.

"He *IS* FISM," the other replies.

"You never heard of FISM, boy?" Gene asks me, but he doesn't give me much time to respond.

"It stands for 'Fuck, It's Still Me,'" he says, "and if you're at double-par, you can pick your ball up and the rest of us actual golfers can finish the hole."

You can take me to fancy golf courses and I can play them. I can pretend to be someone I'm not, and sometimes I succeed. But in the end? Fuck, it's still me.

"Actually, this is only my ninth," I tell Gene with shameful mock pride. I give it my best putt, and the ball passes two other ball markers on its way to the cup, but still falls short. It's no longer a FISM situation, but I'm at double-par. I pick up and head for the next hole.

"I may not know what FISM is, but I know what life is, Gene."

I do not get my name on the purchase order.

PAR: 72   SCORE: 113

A memory plays out like a film sequence in my mind: I pull out the old hand-me-down golf clubs from the Golf Zone in my garage. Payne oozes past like a spectre. Wet and smelling of adolescent hormonal sweat. The odour is relentless. He does what he can. The sheer onslaught of it forces his neck to crane forward and tilts his skull downward, so he gazes at his shoes.

When he was five, I couldn't wait to teach him the game. With such an ample head start, he could be a scratch golfer before anyone expected anything out of him. When he was twelve, he threw the whole golf bag at me. Still, every spring I would break out the clubs and hold one up to show him, the way you might hold a Frisbee up to your dog. His refusals became less emphatic, but more automatic.

Now colonies of rust have found a home on the surface of the metal. I hold one up like I'm performing a solemn tribute to it, hoping that maybe Payne's wet ghost will glide its way over here like a sullen pope and tell me, "Hey, Dad, don't chuck those out yet. There's still hope. Plenty of time for us and that game you're so in love with."

Instead, I say, "You want these clubs?"

"Fuck no," he says, and leaves a sweaty vapour trail on his way downstairs to his bedroom.

The scene ends with the rattle-slam of the clubs plunging into the garbage bin.

I head to the backyard to practice.

2

VICTORIA BEACH, 2016
Manitoba: Nine Holes
Designer Unknown

I make a really poor outside-in swing with the 4-iron, flinging my club face way open, and the ball takes an expressway off-ramp to the right, barely any loft to it at all. I try to keep my eye on it, angling my head and neck like a six-foot-tall, middle-aged meerkat, alert and idiotic, watching the poor launch of my dimpled hopes and dreams, compressed into a sphere. The ball zips beneath the leaves and I am lost.

This course is covered—blanketed—with leaves, catching the light from the September sun in flickers and flashes, deceptively mimicking the bright surface of my golf ball, giving me the confidence to know that I will never find it. I peer up at the shedding trees and beyond them, to every single cloud in the sky, wondering why leaves need to fall in the first place. They sure do mess with my ability to find a shank.

Why does life need to fall from life at all? What is it that nature seeks to accomplish in the leaving of leaves? Like some kind of golf philosopher, I ponder this weird thought as I kick through the brittle sea of yellow and brown, knowing I'll spend five minutes looking futilely for a ball that is already lost.

Do leaves leave a tree? Or does a tree finally leave them be, allowing them their final ride along gravity's welcoming beckon, making their inevitable descent to where they can obscure my ability to find my goddamn golf ball?

If you search the word "leave" on your phone, you'll find out the word originally meant "to remain," to stay the same. I don't get it. If I take my leave of something, I am departing. If leaves leave a tree, they are falling away to their doom. How could its current usage have come to mean the exact opposite of the intended, original meaning of the word?

When you die, you don't get to stay. Everything leaves.

I scroll on my phone: "to give license or permission," from a root word I can't even pronounce that means to care for, to love. *Leubh.*

What a thought, that each of these leaves is granted loving permission by the tree to remain on the ground, where gravity has placed it, to decompose and rot and become peat and then nurture a tree with leaves all over again. Or maybe some Bermuda grass.

I peer over my shoulder and see the twosome behind me catching up. They stand at the tee box, shrugging at one another and eyeing me. They're debating whether to play through. I'm taking too long. Time to let it go.

As soon as I stop looking for it, I spy a flash of white under the ochre of dead leaf. My ball! Easy enough to know if it's mine, since I mark all of them the same way: two letters, an *O* and a *B*, circled in red with a line through it. This is supposed to keep it from going out of bounds. I have had mixed results.

Faith's dad, Chi-Chi, always marked his ball with a solid red, double-thick line, a monolith that matched the man. Today, I play for him. Today, I wish he didn't leave. I'll never golf like he did. Not that he was a legendary golfer or anything: if mastery of this ridiculous game is a life-long process, then Chi-Chi was on the same course, but way ahead, I told myself. That gave me some comfort. The only way I could ever catch up would have been for him to stop getting better.

Now that he's gone, I'm sure I'll never catch up.

I pick up the ball I've uncovered and spin it to confirm that it's mine, but this oldie has been shaved by a lawn-mower blade. I drop the expired ball, committing it back to its final resting place on the golf course, a noble ending for a golf ball. But not the most noble. Chi-Chi's Longest Shot has to be the most noble ending.

I drop a fresh ball, marked with a big, green number seven, written in marker. The seven probably takes up half the ball. I don't recall making this mark, but you find all kinds of things when you rummage through the out-of-bounds areas. Still, who would put a giant seven on their ball, and why? For luck?

I rush the shot and scull a 4-iron into a bunker that really shouldn't be in play at all, but I find a way to make it an obstacle.

"Let's go, hun," Faith's voice calls from ahead of me, and even a scold from my wife sounds like a lullaby, carrying me into another memory.

"Are you for real? Another trip already?" she says.

"I have to do it," I tell her. There's no one holding a gun to my head.

"You told Payne you'd be at his concert this year, hun."

"He won't remember that," I tell her, but it's a poor excuse. I look into her eyes and try to show her how bad I feel about leaving, because we can communicate in passages with our eyes right now. If I could stay in this bed forever, with her, that's what I would do. We are so in love. We have so much in front of us.

I close my eyes and reach out for her, running my index finger along the top of her shoulder, down to the clavicle, tracing the perfect design of her.

"What are you doing?" she says.

I don't open my eyes. I focus on the touch.

"You're feeling me up like a blind perv."

"I'm remembering you, with my fingers," I tell her. "I'll remember every curve the whole time I'm gone."

"James Khoury, what has gotten into you?"

"No, my dear, the question is: what's getting into you?" And we smile, eyes coming as close together as blades of grass.

"James." Her face is cold. She's anxious to continue golfing.

We're on the sixth hole at Victoria Beach, an ancient course carved from the boreal forest that fills this whole peninsula on the east side of Lake Winnipeg.

Victoria Beach is the only place we golf together. But

since Chi-Chi left, we both may as well be golfing on our own.

We come here a lot. Every year we rent a place, try to spend some time together, just Faith, Payne, and me. But every rotation around the sun shows us how our orbits have decayed. The pull weakens. We drift.

On the lengthy seventh hole, there's a big evergreen plunked right in the middle of the fairway. Faith hits the longest drive she's ever managed.

"Wow! Incredible!" My excitement is genuine, and with that one shot I've projected it all out in my hopeful mind: Faith will get on a heater; her confidence will grow; she'll finally love the game as much as I do; we can golf together, like that's some kind of divine communing practice I need to achieve spiritual fulfillment. Yep, I've got it all imagined and now it's becoming a plan.

But Faith covers her face and cries.

I put my hand on her back and ask her what's wrong, even though I know the answer.

"I just wish Dad was here," she says between sniffles. "Go," she tells me, and for a second, I'm not sure if she's telling me to leave or to take my shot.

"Sorry," Faith whispers as I try to look down the fairway. "I try not to cry in front of you."

In front of you. That makes us go quiet.

The rest of the round brings no joy. My fortune-telling turns out to be completely wrong, as always. She plays her normal way, because she doesn't play enough to do any better. She's only here because this is what I love to do. I can see being out here is killing her, but she's trying to make me happy. I ask her if she wants to go, but there are only two holes left. She shakes her head.

On the ninth hole, the round comes to a merciful end. We offer each other a polite nod and a handshake, congratulations on a nice round, and the flag goes back in the hole.

PAR: 35   SCORE: 57

"*That's not how it went.*"

"*That's totally how it did, James, and as usual, you bend your memories to suit you.*" *Her tone is soft but venomous. She's accused me of this so many times, I'm starting to wonder if she actually believes it.*

I think my memory is fantastic. She thinks I'm completely delusional.

I do what I always do: I try to give Faith a play-by-play of exactly how the disputed scenario in question went. It doesn't even matter what the scenario was or how either of us felt about it; all that matters now is whether or not my recounting of the scene is accurate or a completely narcissistic fantasy conjured up by my brain to justify how I already see, think, and feel about things.

I tell the story. Faith's eyes narrow. "You're misremembering." This is how it always goes, and suddenly I'm aware of the grand pattern of things, and I want to smash it with a sledgehammer.

"*Look, this is stupid,*" *I tell her.* "*We're here, I love you and you love me, and we're both alive.*"

"*How dare you,*" *Faith says. She spins around and turns*

on the tap before grabbing a plate and scrubbing it viciously. A cleaner dish has never been produced from our sinks.

Faith stops and studies the suds like she might be able to burst them with a glare. The sun from the window above the sink beams around her, making the edges of her hair glow golden. I slide my arms around her, drawing her against my chest. The water keeps running.

I lean in for a tender kiss on the back of her neck—something light, something to warm her and bring her closer.

She bends her neck. Puts her ear in the way.

"Stop that," she whispers. I think it's playful. Of course I would.

The streaming water fills the air with sound, overwhelming the drain.

I try again. She pretends to wipe the side of her eye with her forearm, but I know it's to twist away from me.

I loosen my grip.

"Trying to do the dishes," she says, but I'm a wraith, already sliding from the room to stop haunting her. Now she can be alone with the ghost she's pining for.

3

CABOT CLIFFS, 2017
Nova Scotia: Eighteen Holes
Bill Coore and Ben Crenshaw

While not necessarily the most exclusive course I've ever played, Cabot Cliffs is certainly the most beautiful. How could it not be, especially for a prairie boy whose jaw drops at the sight of a cliff face or ocean shore?

But it's more than that. This course captures the Maritime spirit. You need a jacket to play here. It'll put the rose on your cheeks and weaken your knees, especially that sixteenth. The younger sibling of Cabot Links, this course has been ranked among the top places to play golf on Earth, giving Cape Breton two of the top tracks in the world. Unfortunately, I can only in good conscience add one extra day to my trip, so I choose Cliffs. Links will have to live on in my dreams.

When I start my round here, Fiona calls me "buddy,"

which is a colloquial term in the area, not unlike "sir" in other parts of Canada. But by the end of the round, she's calling me "b'y," the Maritime version of "boy," a term that would translate to "buddy" or "brother."

It's not the easiest to get here, but I find a way. After struggling to stay awake through a tradeshow in Halifax, I rent a car and head out before dawn the next day. It's four hours, plus Tim's stops, and I get to the front desk just before my ten-thirty tee time.

Big surprise when I get there: the other three golfers I've been grouped with have had their flight cancelled. I'm on my own.

Just me and the caddie.

Cabot Cliffs is a walking course. It is meant to be savoured in the traditional way: on foot. "A walk spoiled," someone once described golf. Historically, only the privileged were afforded the opportunity to swing the clubs and wear the knickers, and they often employed a caddie to do the hard work of carrying their equipment around for them. Of course, anyone who has met a member of the upper class knows that the salt-of-the-earth, down-trodden local will always understand their surroundings in ways the aristocracy could only dream of, and so the caddie also provides knowledge of the local terrain, how conditions affect yardage, how best to attack challenges the landscape doles out, how to win friends and influence people, and other best practices for general life enhancement. In other words, the caddie is no cad. He is a guru.

Or she.

"Fiona," my caddie says to me, offering her hand. I take it and she quickly slides out of my handshake to reach for my bag. Fiona isn't sixty yet, I don't think, but she's lived her fair share if her crow's feet are any indication. She's barely five feet tall and doesn't fill out the massive white overalls the golf club has supplied her. I feel a twinge of guilt for letting her do all this heavy lifting, but then I remember that this is her job, that I'm being sexist for even thinking it, and she is quite capable of doing what she is being paid to do.

I get to enjoy the privilege that is golf at Cabot Cliffs. What a feeling it is. The crisp Atlantic air sharpens my focus and chills my nose.

"You and me today, buddy," Fiona says.

"So I hear."

"You get my undivided attention, so we'll see if you think that's good fortune or not." Fiona winks at me.

We embark, and it takes only two minutes before Cliffs presents its first jaw-dropping vista on the par-5 opening hole, which rolls out like a green runway to the Gulf of Saint Lawrence on the west side of the Cape. I fight the knee-buckling sensation of vertigo with every step, as the course itself feels raised above the ocean like it's been put on a pulpit. The morning sun blazes a cool white cross-hatch onto the somersaulting waves, forcing my eyes away from the gulf and over to the meandering shoreline that slithers off into the distance. Farther south, I see the village of Inverness.

"Such a beautiful place," I say to Fiona.

Fiona gives me a cool gesture with her chin toward one of the white houses way off in the town of Inverness, though there's no chance I could discern which miniature house she's pointing at from such a distance.

"I live in that one," she says.

We stand there, looking at the little prosaic village as the breeze rises up, diminishes, then rises again. I wonder if we're ever going to golf. Finally, Fiona looks into the bag and withdraws my driver.

"Where's home for you?" she asks, and I tell her, with the same shame most Winnipeggers do. Fiona doesn't know how to reply to this piece of tragic news, and so she says, "Family out there?"

The expansive first fairway fills my vision. Even though it gently slopes to the right, there are only two bunkers to watch out for and a ton of open space for my ball to find. I wiggle my club, settling it into my grip. "Sure, yep. Wife and a kid. Any caddie advice for me on this shot?"

"Get it on the fairway? Sorry, caddie humour." I offer her a polite facial expression as she finally casts her gaze upon the golf course. "You have options here. You try and carry that bunker on the right if you believe yourself to be long enough—that's the quickest way to a good look at the green. Otherwise, play it safe and set up a good second shot."

I take my tee and push it into the earth like a syringe, my thumb pressing between index and middle finger. Then I pull back gently with a slight twist to get it exactly to my preferred height, with about one-quarter of the ball visible above the driver. I place my worst ball on the tee because I half-expect to slice this ball right into the ocean.

As I draw back into my backswing, I swear I hear Fiona tut to herself and mutter something. I can't believe it. I lower my club and glare at her.

"I'm sorry," she says.

I raise an eyebrow. Major etiquette breach.

"My fault. Please, go ahead."

I sigh and return to my swing, but I don't get far before Fiona interjects: "It's just that you focus on the wrong things, is all."

"This is going to dramatically affect your tip, Fiona."

"Sorry, it slipped out."

"What should I focus on, Fiona? Your tutting?"

"Please, go ahead. Enjoy your round."

We become friends about midway through the round, as the course moves uphill from the low-lying sand dunes. When I finally admit—to both Fiona and myself—that I can't golf worth a damn, we both relax.

I suspect relaxing helps one's golf game. I hope to experience this miraculous transformation one day.

The ninth hole is a curt par-3 that makes it look like you're going to spill the ball into the ocean if you even get close to sticking the green. And so, being the golfer I am, I start my ball left. Using nothing more than a gap wedge, I lay all of my metaphysical intent on this ball marked with a big green seven. The ball obeys at first, then relents to the forces of nature and poor spin control, slicing to the right and straight into one of the most punitive bunkers I've ever seen, dark and moist with ochre sand. From where we stand, I can tell the ball is plugged right in, buried up to its neck.

"Bad golf is better than no golf, right?" I offer. Since the incident at the first hole, Fiona and I have been all business. She's been regurgitating scripted snippets of what to look out for on each hole, like a recently trained tour guide. The descriptions don't add to the beauty, but then, not much could. Even on a less-than-ideal-weather day like today, Cabot Cliffs reminds you that there is beauty in resolve; toughness is as much of a virtue as tenderness, and you need both in these parts.

Fiona smiles in response to my self-deprecating quip and it lights up her crow's feet. I see wisdom in her face.

Honestly, outside of the magical characteristics of golf, I don't believe in anything else that I can't see. But as I recall this moment, clutching my desecrated Cabot Cliffs shirt in the Hall of Fame, the lobster logo ripped right out of it, a feeling comes over me. It's like an intuition, that I should listen to what Fiona has to say, because Fiona has something to offer me.

So as we walk to the bunker, I ask her if she's been a caddie her whole life.

She laughs. "I've been telling people what they should do and toting around their crap for a long time, but this is my second year doing this. How about you, James Khoury?"

"I'm a salesman. I work for a major forest products corporation, peddling dead trees to people around the world. It gets me to a lot of good golf courses."

"Surely your family must miss you, on the road so much," Fiona says.

"I'm sure they get enough of me when I'm home," I tell her, not fully believing my own words.

Fiona walks up to the edge of the bunker and studies my ball. She gets up close, crouching to look at its position, midway up the side of the trap. Of its own accord, the ball pops out of the sand and rolls down to a much more playable lie.

Fiona looks at me with wonderment.

I look back at her with a grin and a happy shrug.

"Ah," Fiona says to me. "A natural correction. Take advantage, James Khoury."

And I do, managing to save par with a pitch onto the green and a nice ten-foot putt. The ball makes a metallic *tink* in the cup; one of the things that separates this place from all the others is when you sink your putt, it sounds like you're hitting the hull of a fishing trawler.

Fiona slaps me a high five.

I try not to remember the next few holes and how disastrous each stroke and score feels. My mind is everywhere, it seems. There's so much to take in. I turn away from my view of Margaree Island, sitting in the ocean past the fifteenth green like a great green whale, pestered by white birds which, Fiona informs me, are cormorants.

From that incredible vista, I turn to see the most majestic golf hole in all of Canada, and perhaps the world: the sixteenth hole at Cabot Cliffs.

If I believed that God was a golf course designer, perhaps working through the hands and hearts of mortals, the sixteenth at Cliffs would be my key piece of evidence. It is as though the earth itself rose up and out of the ocean to offer up this par-3 challenge. Where I stand, one hundred and seventy-six yards from the green, I can see a top of a flag, but the green itself is elevated enough that it isn't clearly visible. What I can see is a not-insignificant sand trap staring me in the face, then the flag, and then the lip of another sand trap. Sand trap sandwich.

We take a path from behind the tee box to gain a better

vantage point, but most of my vision is filled with cliff. Rocky crags dominate my sightline as I peer over the edge. Ocean waves lap up against an unfettered beach that represents a beeline from me to the pin. Some kind of white seafaring bird—osprey, or albatross maybe?—flies along the rockface below the hole, nesting in the crags a good hundred feet *beneath the hole!*

If I lay up to the left and try to survive this hole instead of scoring an unlikely good score, the ball could still go in any number of directions. The green sits beneath whatever's on the left. Fairway? Green? I can't quite tell.

"The green here is the biggest you'll see," Fiona says. "If the pin was back and left, you'd have a much tougher time. But you're in luck today; it's off to the right, so fill your boots."

"Luck is not what I'm feeling right now."

Okay, Most Beautiful Golf Hole in the World, I'm going to play you. I set up, waggling side to side, like a cat preparing to pounce, and then inch my feet into exactly the correct spot. I take aim, trying to push thoughts of the cliffs and ocean out of my mind. *Optimism, James. Optimism.* If I slice it and it spins off to the right, the ball is gone. If I leave it short, it's gone. If I push it left, Fiona tells me I could be putting from a hundred feet away, or more. I push left to accommodate the not-so-slight possibility that a slice is going to happen. I open my stance a hair, turning my left hip away from the gulf.

"See. That's exactly what I'm talking about," Fiona says, in the exact moment I'm about to pull my club back. I abort the swing and turn to face her.

"I'm sorry?"

"You focus on missing the trouble."

I gesture toward the cliffs, trying not to raise my voice. "The trouble is over there, so I'm going to avoid going over there, thanks."

"But if you stay focused on over there, you're not focused on over here."

"So meta," I tell her, a forbidden word for me to use, according to Payne. "Can I play?"

She goes on: "I'm telling you, worry about what's next and you don't consider where you are."

"Okay, Fiona," I say as I withdraw my 5-iron from the bag. "I'm thinking about nothing but right here, right now, and this shot. Here is my club, and my ball and my tee. Now what?"

"I don't think you have a lot of choice but to take the shot, do you? Got to be here but you don't get to stay here. Other people need the tee box, right?"

"I'm starting to smell some golf-life metaphor, Fiona." I waggle and prepare to shoot.

"Well that's why, is it not?" she says.

"I'm sorry?"

"Why would we spend so much time golfing if it's not loaded with metaphor? If it doesn't tell you something about your authentic self?"

A sudden pang hits my stomach, like a drop of liquid dye into a pot of water, clouding everything, changing its nature. It's not unlike the mixture of shame and dread I've felt in a moment of FISM.

I don't want golf to say anything about me.

Suddenly, I need to know what Faith is doing right now, if she's at home or out shopping, or maybe weeding the garden. I wonder if Payne is in school, napping, or hanging out with his friends at the Sev, or whatever the teenage boy equivalent is, nowadays.

But there's something else. The feeling in my gut intensifies. It grows and darkens like a yawning sinkhole that ends in infinity, and at its precipice a city worker has diligently placed a warning sign, admonishing the citizen who thought about peering over its edge and falling in.

I'm supposed to remember something important about my family. Something I'm not remembering.

I heed the warning sign and stop peering over the edge, into the metaphorical pit. I pull myself out and focus on what's here: a golf ball that is going to be a permanent resident at the most majestic-looking golf hole in the world.

"There's a big difference between golf and life, Fiona," I tell her. "Sometimes, in golf, I like to believe that I'm in control."

"It's fun to hit a ball sometimes," Fiona says. "Something different to believe you've got some sway over the forces of nature, b'y."

I swing the club. The contact feels clean, but a stiff Atlantic wind gusts into my face. I lose track of the ball in the glare of the sun, so I turn to Fiona to see where she's looking. Her face seems to register some satisfaction.

She hands me the putter and says, "You're putting from there."

I have a spring in my stride, like the pros on TV. I make the long walk to my ball with only my putter in hand.

My tee shot lands on the far left, well above the green. My putt needs to run over a hundred feet; easily the longest putt I'll ever make.

"What should I do?" I ask Fiona, hoping she'll give me the green's tendency to break left and right and by how much. There's a mound in my way, to confound matters.

"Get the ball in the hole."

"That's your expert opinion? You got a PhD in caddying with that kind of sage advice?"

"Sure."

The shot feels like an arcade game. I send the ball down the hill with a leftward break, and then up the mound it goes, and then back down, breaking right. It comes to rest with the bottom of its big green seven pointing at the cup like a finger gun. It's still twelve feet away.

"James Khoury sounds like a made-up name," Fiona says.

"All names are made up," I reply as I kneel to study the next putt.

"My family name was Saad," and I spell it out for her. "Family legend has it that my great-grandfather did something so terrible that he was exiled from his family in Syria and took a new name when he got here. *Et voilà.*"

"What's the terrible thing he did?"

"No one remembers."

"Lost to the tides," Fiona says.

That triggers a flash of a befuddling memory from Victoria Beach.

Faith sits atop the largest rock on King Edward Beach, the closest beach to our cottage. As I approach, the setting sun turns her into a silhouette, long and languid. Every divot from every footstep in the sand has a shadow from the dying sun, a shadow that fills it half-full and leaves it half-empty. The waves run cold as the Lake Winnipeg tide rises, polishing all the tiny rocks in its grasp, rolling them up and down the shore. Pulling a few back into the deep.

Faith missed dinner.

As I trudge closer, I see that her ashen blonde hair covers her face as she curls her arms around herself, convulsing through a paroxysm of emotional electrocution.

"What's wrong?" I ask, even though I know her answer. "I'm here, babe," I say to her, but it doesn't get through. I'm not golfing, I'm not working, I'm not anything, but Faith is above me, waiting to get pulled out by the tide. Hoping to be the next pebble.

I'm not there. I'm here, thousands of miles away, transported by memory from memory, and all I want to do is forget my life for half a second.

Instead, I forget to pay attention as I sink my ball for the par-3 on the sixteenth. I'm indifferent to the majesty of the cliffs on seventeen and sputter to a finish on the final hole. I reach into my wallet for a tip at the end of the round, but Fiona refuses it.

"I was telling you, focus on the right thing. You weren't focused on anything," she says. And she's right.

PAR: 72   SCORE: 102

"There it is again," Faith says through gritted teeth. "The silent treatment."

It's not a silent treatment. I'm not trying to administer anything. I'm in the bottom of a pit, so far away from words. No words would fix this anyway.

I'm paralyzed. I'm thinking of four thousand things to

say at once and none of them are safe. None of them won't hurt or might be something I'm thinking because I'm red. Everything is coloured red and I don't know if what I'm thinking is real, so if I say it, I might ruin everything and Faith will take her love away and so my brain can't make my mouth move. Better to say nothing.

The clock pounds out every second, and suddenly I hate the clock and make a note to buy a new one that doesn't sound like a forging hammer on an anvil sixty times a minute.

"You wonder where Payne gets it from," Faith says to me and she crosses her arms. Stares out the bay window.

There's a golf course out there, I think to myself; green and tranquil among the red cacophony of everything else.

"Don't you realize how much it hurts me when you shut off like this?" she says, her face reddening. Hardening.

I open my mouth but nothing comes out, because I know she's right. I can't risk it. I can't pick one of the things I'm thinking and know it's what I should say and then say it.

If only she could hold me. If only she could wrap her arms around me and say, "Just talk. I won't react. I will never be hurt. You let it out and there will be no unintended consequences."

But she doesn't. That's not how we work.

"Makes me even sadder," Faith says. We go lower.

I wish I could take her with me, to golf and simply live. Somewhere fancy and well-appointed. Somewhere the greens run true and fast. Where the only comfort we need is to play golf with each other.

4

The crest on my green Tobiano shirt is a tall rectangle, meant to look like a classic, antique picture frame, with a stylized, oblong *T* in the centre. Closer inspection shows the *T* to actually be two rotated *L*s, each with serifs at the tip to further add to the unique look of the Tobiano *T*.

The crest is a muted golden colour, which works well on the two-toned green fabric. That timeless-looking letter *T*, set in an ornamental frame, is emblematic of the course itself. Thomas McBroom did some of his best work here, finding ways to give me a view of Kamloops Lake at every hole, somehow running this course through the terrain of the BC interior in a manner that is surprising, yet inevitable, like the way all the best movies end.

"We don't sell lumber," I told my guys the day before.

"We are giving people the tools to shape nature itself." All twelve faces staring back at me were completely blank. I thought maybe Krista would pick up what I was trying to put down, but she looked as nonplussed as the others. So I wrote something on the whiteboard that a dozen people wired up to sell things could understand: *Trees = Dreams. Dreams = $$$.*

Widespread nodding.

The sales team meetings always end in a round of golf, and we're all excited to try Tobiano, widely regarded as the best public golf course in BC. So as the last item of our rah-rah-get-your-numbers-up-third-place-is-you're-fired type of meeting, I draw names to determine our playing groups.

I pull my own name out in a group with Darryl, the new guy Rhodes, and the last remaining name in the hat, Krista.

As I rest my hands on the power cart, waiting for Krista to load her bag, I notice how the summer's sun has given me a tan. I stretch my fingers out to examine them. I left my ring at home. Again.

Krista sits down and announces she's ready. I stomp on the gas pedal and the cart hesitates for a second, like it's having a thought, and then lurches toward the first hole.

British Columbia has a reputation for being humid—no, waterlogged—because of its proximity to the ocean, but the interior is arid and warm, and can sometimes be the hottest place in all of Canada. Tobiano's well-maintained greenery is framed by the browns and yellows of the native tall grasses and brush of Thompson Country. It makes the fertile landscape seem even more so.

From the intimidating first tee box, it's a long way down to the three bunkers that warn you not to over-hit on this par-5.

"Wonderful day for terrible golf," I say to Krista, and she smiles. She's been working for me for about two years now. She holds her own in a traditional male setting, to be sure. I wonder how much of it is a mask she's had to put on to survive.

"Terrible golf's better than no golf at all, right?" she says to me, showing her knack for saying exactly the right thing. It's helped Krista find her place in this company; that and her unrivalled ability to sell forest products. She's been second to me in sales for the past six months, and now she's giving me a run for top spot. The competition is friendly, though.

Krista spins a tee and it falls to the grass. The tee points at the new guy, Rhodes, giving him the honour. Without asking, he strides back to the "tournament" tees, marked by two earth-tone cubes, the farthest back of the five tees.

I almost say something.

Rhodes creates one of those awful grab-your-package male machismo situations, like a dog presenting itself to a male competitor, and I am obliged by some kind of idiotic gender norm to also hit from twenty-five yards back, at the tournament tees. In golf parlance, it's called "playing from the tips."

Not only is it expected that the men are to play with the men, it's also more efficient. Golfers need to stay parallel with their playing partners, and it reduces the number of starts and stops per hole when you're driving a power cart by a grand aggregate total of one.

None of us have ever seen Rhodes swing a golf club before. We're all impressed. He looks like a pro in the set-up and Darryl emits a "whoa" as Rhodes cranks his drive, virtually straight at those three bunkers below us that hug the right side of the fairway as it sweeps left. It must be three hundred yards.

"Nope," Rhodes says as he watches his ball roll right into the beach. He's disappointed.

Even if I teed off from the middle "spur" tees, I can't reach that distance. I know it shouldn't, but it equates to my perceived self-worth as a man.

Thank God I'm not the next one up.

Darryl's a long-time floater on my team. Nice guy, but not physically fit at all, not the sharpest tool in the toolbox, shed, or hardware store, and barely capable enough as a salesman to avoid termination. But he makes his quota every month.

No one would accuse Darryl of being thoughtful. He spends exactly zero seconds considering whether he should tee off from the tournament tees. He walks up there and gives 'er, and like everything else about him, Darryl's swing is barely good enough. It's compact and he doesn't bother trying to move his follow-through around his rye-drinker's belly. But the ball gets up in the air, short and aimed incorrectly, and lands in the right rough, seventy-five yards shy of Rhodes's.

Resigned to giving in to the pressure of binary gender expectations, I make my death row march to the back tees. I push the air out of me.

"You got this, boss. Let's go," Krista says. That makes me feel worse because I know I don't got this. Not in the slightest.

I recall the words of Fiona, the Cabot Cliffs caddie: "Focus on where you're at," or something along those lines is what she advised me, right? Where I'm at is a starting point thirty yards behind where I would like to be. *How does that help, Fiona? Focus on my unfair starting point?*

I push Fiona out of my mind. I calm myself down, tell myself to prepare carefully, quiet my thoughts. Even though they're my employees, I know they're observing my every move, and the sensation of being watched changes my behaviour. I'm simultaneously golfing and not golfing. I can't be truly within myself, focused on the right thing, as Fiona would say. I'm inauthentic.

Push it all out, I tell myself. *Stop thinking.* But the resulting vacuum draws in thoughts of Faith again. Our most recent argument. She was angry with me. Angry because of Payne.

I step away from the tee and take a walk around. Line it all up again. Push my family away in my mind, as I have in every other way. I mean, it's one of the great things about golf, right? If I'm here, I'm not there.

This particular ball has a long, narrow line drawn along its equator, perfectly straight, like someone used a stencil or a vise to draw it. I hear some people use this trick to help their putting.

I stare at a single, solitary dimple along that black line, draw my driver back slowly and try to maintain that out-stretched arm and a hinged wrist. I'm focused on where I am—this paradise, this symbiosis of man and nature laid out like a Rorschach test for those who play it—which is gloriously disconnected from my world. Everything stands impossibly still.

Down comes the club and the swing feels smooth. I

brush the tee out of the turf and the ball sails straight and high, looking mighty darn good, almost regal, as it arcs like a rainbow and lands on the rolling hills of the fairway, close to the centre, two-hundred-plus yards away and looking safe down there. The ball rockets up the side of a hill, returns to flight briefly ... but then falls down the side of that same hill, flipping Isaac Newton the bird as it gains enough reverse momentum to roll over the crest of the previous hill on the fairway.

My neck and shoulder radiate electric zots of pain up to the top of my left ear and down to my pinkie finger. Nerve pinch. It feels like a two-hundred-pound bee stings me in the place where my neck meets my shoulder. And in that sting, I remember Faith, and what she shouted at me the day we came together.

"WATCH—"

I met Faith in my second year of university. She was aloof and modest but a knockout, completely oblivious to all the attention she was getting from male classmates and even faculty. I'm sure this is not uncommon for a woman whose eyes have a sparkle of innocence, who believes the world is fundamentally good, and who has never wanted for attention, but with Faith it went beyond that. She'd never seen herself as an object of desire, or even as desirable. It goes beyond modesty with Faith, and I guess my job since we got together has always been to hold up a mirror, to show her how beautiful she is, inside and out.

As for me, I probably fell in love with her the first minute we met, in Microeconomics, where she barely concealed her disdain for consumerism, aspiring to live somewhere above it, holding humanity to a higher account than Adam Smith ever did.

Not that I said anything to her. But I knew who Faith was and I saw her, truly saw her, every Monday, Wednesday, and Friday at 8:50 a.m. to 9:40 a.m., and I let her go ahead of me in the coffee line before class where we exchanged smiles, and I was smitten with the way she looked down at her own feet. It made her look overwhelmed by the world, maybe in disbelief that her feet had taken her all the way here. After watching her do this for some weeks, I began looking down at my own feet too.

Unfortunately for me, there were always other boys around, and I had such little game, so I would never approach her. I assumed that Faith had her choice of whom to date. That included several of the boys whose lives had recently peaked, and now they were scrambling to hold on to every follicle of their high school prominence; they needed to put forth an effort to show they had become somewhat human and adult in their thinking, and Faith seemed to draw them into her world like a diviner. I watched some of those guys try mightily to win even a hint of attention from her, or to try and match wits. The last thing I was going to do, as a twenty-year-old virgin from the murder part of town, who still wore a retainer and carried tiny scars from freshly popped pimples, was try to compete with the lettermen.

Then there was that one guy.

"Hey, you should come to the Aggies' social. It's going to be epic."

Faith doesn't even look up from her notebook, which contains a wonderland of spindly doodles: cubes, arrows, a

*Medusa's head, every currency symbol she can think of, an
ant. A near-perfect sphere.*

"Epic?" She asks.

*The letterman bares his teeth. "Yeah. It's a totally crazy
time. We should totally—"*

"Crazy or epic? Which one?" She still doesn't look up.

*Uh-oh. "Uhhh ... epic, I guess?" The letterman is on the
ropes.*

*"I think you and I are into different Homers," she tells the
guy, and I was the only one who got it.*

*Faith hears me giggle. It's the first time she looks at me
and the look goes deep.*

Ten years later, I met Faith again. I needed every minute of that decade to screw up and collect battle scars and
understand people and the world, at least enough so that I
might have a puncher's chance to keep a relationship alive
for more than three months.

For some people, falling in love feels like they got hit by
a truck. I actually did get hit by a truck.

I was crossing the street downtown when I heard a
voice behind me, soft and lyrical and I knew who she was,
even though I hadn't heard her voice in a decade.

"James?" I stopped mid-street. "James Khoury, right?"
I turned around.

There she was, now thirty, the decade changing her
face the way a low tide leaves the finest beach sand. The
sun had washed her with a golden tan. Inside, I scram-
bled to look cool and nonchalant: *how the hell does she
know my name?* I looked past her left shoulder, then her
right, as though someone else may have sung my name
and made my spine quiver. I pointed toward her with the

softest index finger and tried to flash a facial expression that showed I was casual and not flabbergasted, and managed to utter, "Faith? Faith, right?"

She told me later she planned to say "I knew your brother and I'm so sorry," but instead she shouted, "WATCH—" as a black tidal wave of unconsciousness came at me, from my right to left, like a TV show changing scenes with a wipe. There wasn't any pain, just a state of dreamy annoyance that my reunion with Faith was interrupted and I didn't get to hear what she was going to say. Apparently a slow-moving garbage truck clipped me because I was standing in the middle of moving traffic. Slow-moving, but a garbage truck, nonetheless.

When I came to, I was in the hospital, getting checked for a concussion and internal bleeding. The doctors said the garbage truck tenderized me, but they couldn't find anything wrong. No cracks on the X-ray. Faith had cared for me so well out on the street that nothing serious had happened to me. Nothing serious, except for meeting my wife.

Faith was at my side in that hospital and would never leave it again.

"Next time, get hit by an ice cream truck," she said to me with that wry half-smile of hers, melting me instantly.

But right now, at Tobiano, I'm thinking too much, and about the wrong thing. My hand trembles and a scorpion's kiss of pain travels from my shoulder down to my fingertips. Up ahead, Krista readies her tee shot.

"This course is incredible," she says to me. "Don't you love golf?"

A few holes later, as we drive between the eighth and ninth, Krista says to me, "You're in pain, aren't you?"

I'm doing a shit job of hiding it. My left arm feels dead from the shoulder down, and it's affecting my game.

"Anything I can do, boss?" she says to me.

I look at her. She's offering to give me a massage, I think. She's my employee.

After a moment that is probably longer than it should be, I shake my head.

This round is awful for me. I play embarrassingly bad golf in front of my staff, but they are quite charitable in their praise of my efforts. Rhodes could have been a pro, the way he's playing. But even Darryl is doing better than I am. Krista is only a stroke or two higher than Rhodes.

After an hour, the stinger subsides, and so pain is not an excuse for me anymore. I'm not in control of my body today.

I rest my best golf ball on the tenth tee. It's a glimmering, clean ball that says "distance" somewhere on it, like a serenity prayer. Suddenly, everything external to me is shut out of my being and I am present, as Fiona coached me to be. Although my face is at least five feet above the ball, my consciousness is hovering about two inches above it. The shimmering dimples fill my view until all I can see is the ball and that hopeful "distance" tattoo. It sits right there awaiting my action upon it. My legs and glutes waggle and lock into a striking position. My left shoulder comes down and the right draws up, my awareness transfixed on this shining white emissary of mine, and the metal rod in my hands becomes a whip, a scythe, a hammer, a sickle, the stars and stripes, the ark of the covenant I've made with myself to become something better—a better golfer, a better liver of life—and this is the hardest tee shot I've ever hit ...

Hitting the ball is not like hitting a nail into a piece of wood. It's not about trying to break through some kind of resistance. The worst a person can do is swing "hard." If I swing hard, I tense my muscles to the point where they don't move quickly, languidly, or with precision; if I swing hard, I pull all kinds of other, connected muscles in directions the hard-swinging muscles are leading them. I would pull myself out of alignment and end up looking like a complete novice, twisting in a spasmodic yoga of idiocy.

If I swing hard, I'm also going to slam the head of my driver into the immaculate turf of Tobiano Golf Course, scarring Earth itself with my failed intentions, making me unwelcome around these parts. The impact will spin the head of said driver in such a way that the backside of the implement will assault the ground once more, prior to the club finally making contact with my brand new ball that prays for distance to somehow be a product of all of this gore. The ball's tattooed wish comes true as it springs from the top of my driver and sends itself on a mission of mercy to Kamloops Lake, leaving a crater in the top of my three-hundred-and-fifty-dollar club that I have swung so very, very hard.

I witness all of it, entirely present and in the moment for one hundred percent of it and with no distractions. It is the authentic me. I witness the absence of earth I've created on the tenth tee box, and I'm present for all of it. Success, Fiona!

I hit the Earth very, very hard.

It seems determined to continue, unabated.

We get to the fourteenth, one of the signature holes at Tobiano. It's at the highest point on the course, and when you tee off, you get to take all of it in: the Rocky Mountain backdrop, then Kamloops Lake, and a green that seems to spill right into the lake, some four hundred and forty yards away. At the base of the mountain range, a long freight train slithers its way along the track. It's like McBroom had scheduled it himself, a final touch to his design ensuring this image is engraved on our memories indelibly.

"This is absolutely majestic," I tell Krista as we ride to our second shots. "I love the design of it."

She nods at me, then looks back out at the vista, like she's appreciating it anew. "Yeah."

"I don't quite know the metaphor I'm going for here," I tell her, "but it's nature and yet human at the same time. This golf course is an expression.".

Krista thinks on that as we approach her ball, sitting atop a mound on the fairway. I bring the cart to a stop, and she surprises me by saying, "I'm not so sure about that."

She hops out and withdraws a club from the back. "It's about us, don't you think?"

"What do you mean?"

"The course is a venue for us to express ourselves," Krista says, addressing her ball.

"So what is it we need to express?" I don't fully appreciate my words until after I've said them.

Krista takes her swing. She's athletic and supple, and her swing is honed. The shot is graceful and sounds fertile and full, like taking a bite from an apple; Krista freezes on the follow-through, her right calf flexed and golf spikes exposed as she digs her toe into the ground.

"It's like we make love with our golfing," she says, bending over to patch the divot she's made in the turf. "Golf is an intimate expression," she adds, like she's only now decided it. "An act of love-making."

I look down at my golf balls, placed in the cup holders on the dash. I study their markings closely.

"Hopefully your intent is loving," Krista says. She walks back to the cart and stops behind me to sheath her club. She pauses for a beat.

"If the earth is the bed, this golf course would be the satin sheets," she says, then chuckles to herself and sits down beside me. Suddenly, the golf cart seems extremely narrow, and as Krista looks out at this vista we're so privileged to be playing in front of, she grasps the handle above her head. Our thighs are forced to brush together ever so slightly. I realize that I have lost my focus on golf entirely.

PAR: 72   SCORE: 113

"Flight, condo, golf, all paid for. You should come."

Faith shakes her head. "Too fancy for me." She pokes at something on her screen. A piece of candy, probably.

"You don't need to be a good golfer to play good courses, Faith. God knows."

She looks up at me with her lemon face. It amazes me what effect that face has on me, as though she points her expression into me like some kind of chisel. I'm not sure if it's because of her years of practice or experience, but I am so easy to carve. So easily affected by her.

"I'm going to embarrass myself," she complains. "You go. It's fine."

"You can get out of here, Faith. You can have an escape for a couple of days. With me." Those words ring hollow in my own ears. She can't escape if she's with me, I bet.

She barely even shakes her head, but musters enough strength to purse her lips and manages a zombie-like "I'm good" before returning to her screen and candy game.

I know it's not good, but I go anyway.

5

DEVIL'S PULPIT, 2018
Ontario: Eighteen Holes
Chris Haney and Dr. Col. Michael Hurdzan

We can see the CN Tower from the first hole, jabbing the sky like the middle finger of Toronto, piercing the serenity of the golf course.

It's me and Rhodes playing this round, and we're both excited to finally be at Devil's Pulpit, which has been one of the top-rated courses in Canada since four PGA pros played the first nationally-televised Canadian skins game here back in the early nineties. Maybe 1993? My memory isn't what it used to be.

A failing memory makes you bad at trivia, and trivia is what built the Devil's Pulpit; the owners are also the inventors of the board game Trivial Pursuit. And that may be the only piece of trivia that I have retained over the years.

Rhodes is a handsome thirty-five-year-old with rusty

hair and some freckles, the lean physique of a swimmer—
all toned and such—with Oakley-shaped tan lines around
his eyes. It all fits together when he puts on the sunglasses
and orange, flat-brimmed cap, fishes out his brand new
clubs, and meets me at the tees.

Rhodes isn't the best salesman, but man, can this kid
hit a ball.

I consider myself serious about my golf, despite how
poorly I play. Rhodes is at a different level entirely. He has
the same easy confidence as Faith's father, Chi-Chi—an
athletic air which I do not possess. Nothing comes easy to
me, not the way it does for Rhodes, or for Chi-Chi. People
like Rhodes and Chi-Chi have killer instincts and aggres-
sion baked right in. The only thing I have baked in is a lot
of shortening.

I can see Rhodes stealing glances at my swing on the
sly as we begin play, and the observation makes me golf
as badly as I usually do: consistently inconsistent and deadly
serious about my reactions and considerations, talking
through the game and making decisions aloud as though
I'm consulting an invisible caddie. I hit a couple of shots so
fat that my club digs up turf like a trowel, and the resulting
impact vibrations radiate up my wrists and arms, reigniting
the pain in my shoulder from Tobiano a few months prior.

Meanwhile, every time I look, Rhodes is in mid-swing,
and it's light, easy, and effortless; perfect vintage form, with
the Gary Player knee bend and pointy toe, made famous
by the PGA Tour logo. He takes no time at all to prepare or
set up. He just does it, like it's breathing, and it's achingly
beautiful to see how naturally golf comes to him.

I've taken lessons before, but every time I do, they have

the opposite effect. You learn, over time, there is no right way to do anything in golf. There's theory and there's tradition, and what works for some lanky, lifelong athlete who plays daily will not work for a cubicle-bound working man hurtling toward middle age like an epoch-ending asteroid. But Rhodes golfs like he knows a secret or two. I can't help myself.

"What do you think about giving me some pointers, Rhodesy? Let's make this a learning round."

Rhodes nods, but he doesn't look too enthused about giving me a lesson.

"You and I both know I could use it."

"I don't know, Jim ..."

"Okay, okay." I give him the "hands-off" gesture. I can't tell my employee to give me a free lesson.

"Tell you what," Rhodes says, "if I see anything I can help with, I'll let you know."

"Fair enough. Appreciate that."

Rhodes's lessons begin at the sixth hole.

Every tee box at Devil's Pulpit has a stone totem next to it, bearing a metal plaque that states the name they've given each hole, along with a description. This one is called "Memorial." Off a titch left of the fairway, in the crook of a sharp left dogleg, stands a square of six maples. As we drive closer, a wrought-iron fence makes itself visible, and inside the fence, we see the gravestones.

Before there was a golf course resting atop the earth here, there was a homestead, and it belonged to the Harris family. In 1861, four Harris children died of diphtheria over the course of a few days, and here they lie, beneath us, a reminder that we golf on the surface as members of the living, propped up by what's buried. They built a golf course around their gravestones. A memorial.

All of the bodies we walk on top of as we duff our way around life ... I think of Chi-Chi. Of my brother, Lane. I stare at my golf shoes as I walk to my ball.

After a painful, clunky shot that farts off the club and spirals a hundred yards, Rhodes can't help himself. I can tell he's got to say something about it.

"Easy adjustment for you to try," he says as we approach my FISM shot. Rhodes drove his ball probably a hundred yards ahead of mine. I try to look eager to learn, but a part of me hopes it's more concrete than "focus on the right thing" or some other weird mantra.

"Take your approach," he says, and I comply, sitting in my stance and stretching out with my 7-iron, the old comfort club.

"Nope," Rhodes tells me, "you're reaching way out. Why do you reach when you could bring it close and hold it strong? Do you understand me?"

"Not really."

He demonstrates with his own club, standing right across from me, and shows me how he keeps his hands closer to his body right from the start of his set-up. He shakes his club for effect. "Here. Much stronger. The ball doesn't need to be so far away from you, and you're better in all aspects when you hold it in close. It's all in your hands."

There's a moment where Rhodes waits expectantly for me to try his way and I don't. I'm not sure I buy what he's telling me.

"But I always thought if I lengthen like this I make a

longer radius, with my arm and club together, and that's going to generate more speed, right? Isn't that true? Wider circle?"

Rhodes looks miffed that I would question him. "I don't know, James. How's your knowledge of geometry working out for you so far?"

"Yeah, but it's science."

"Let's leave science to the scientists, okay? Now how about it? Bring it in close, hold it strong, and don't over-reach. Use the big muscles in your shoulders and back."

I give it a try and notice how much stronger my arms feel as soon as I start my compressed backswing.

"Good. Okay. If you come down, like this, at a low enough angle, it's going to help you hit a draw." Rhodes demonstrates with his two hands, leaving his club resting between his legs.

A draw! Now I'm excited. A right-to-left motion to your shot is supposed to generate distance, or so I've read. I thought that players who could hit a draw were simply born with the ability, like how some people are born telekinetic or clairvoyant. I am neither of these things, and did not once consider that I might someday acquire the ability to bend metal spoons with the power of my mind. I also didn't ever think I could hit a draw with consistency. If Rhodes can show me how to do that, I'll be forever changed.

"You think you can teach me to hit a draw? Today?"

"I taught my son yesterday and he's ten," Rhodes says. "We should get moving, though. Why don't you take this shot and see how reducing the over-reach feels, then we've got some time."

"Right." I pull my hands in toward myself and size up

the flagstick. Instead of one long, straight line from my shoulders to the club head, I see the club coming out at forty-five degrees. The angle of the club face finds a way to make more sense in how it relates to the surface of the earth. The shaft is pointed right at my navel, like a steel umbilical cord.

"Ease back," Rhodes says gently, and I slow my back-swing down like it was being too loud. I visualize this ball catapulting straight into the sky, with authority and per-fection, and I bring my swing down with those tightly held arms, so much easier, but with my right elbow jammed into my ribs.

My club head excavates a hole in the fairway deep enough to bury a woodland creature. I make contact with that nerve in my shoulder-neck area and it burns badly enough that I need to reach for it and rub. I miss the ball completely.

"The new medicine's taking effect," Rhodes says. "Give it time. Try again," said in a tone I'm sure he would have used on his ten-year-old son.

I'm not sure I *can* try again. My arm feels dead and waves of heat are passing through the right side of my body, emanating from the neck and shoulder. I need a second and I think Rhodes knows it. I look back to con-ceal the pained expression on my face, and see a pair of golf carts pulling up to the tees. There used to be no one behind us.

I try again. I can't swing the club gracefully at all and I hit a holy roller that doesn't get two feet above the ground.

"I see it," Rhodes says. "On the fairway."

I cobble together a double-par on Memorial. Rhodes tells me to stop keeping score.

"How old's the boy now?" Rhodes asks me.

"Fifteen," I tell him.

"Teenager," he says. "Good times."

"Sweaty and awkward and smelly and belligerent. It's the worst."

I don't mention to Rhodes how much living with a teenager feels like a decade-long goodbye to the child you've been raising. You know he's going to leave. I don't tell Rhodes how much that hurts. I don't tell him how I miss Payne already, like a part of my son is already gone.

Suddenly there's a strange pang in my mind, like when you know you're supposed to pick something up at the grocery store and you're standing in the middle of an aisle and you can't remember what it is that you came in to buy. I'm supposed to know something about Payne. Something important.

"Can we go home? Please?"

I'm at Victoria Beach, trying to teach Payne how to golf. It's Junior Day, just one dollar for kids to play so long as they hit from the junior tees, each a hundred and fifty yards from the green. Payne is frustrated and I know it. My rage is boiling over too, and I try to show him how to hit the ball, but he can't quite get it.

"Everybody else is at the beach, Dad. This is dumb."

"You're not everybody else, Payne. Trust me. You will thank me later for this."

"I hate you," Payne spits at me. He takes his ball, marked with a pink heart by his mother, and throws it into the forest.

My chance to golf with my boy is lost in the woods. I send him home and finish the round.

I don't know how long I've been silent, but it comes off as an expectant pause, and so Rhodes says, "Hey. We've got our privileges and we've got our tales of woe. Maybe having a kid is both."

I look down. The golf ball is at the end of my club, with a single thick line around its equator, and I hold my 8-iron the Rhodesy way as he leans on his club with one leg crossed, like a human Norman Rockwell painting, smiling at me in this prosaic moment of tranquility and privilege. I hold it in close.

This is an earned privilege for me, this golf. This escape. Maybe it's a privilege and a tale of woe too.

I ease back, but then I ease forward as well. I keep my chin unwavering as the centre of a circle my swing creates. It works. The ball feels like a boiled egg with the shell removed as the contact travels from the club face up the shaft and into my palms; a delicious, delightful sensation of ease, so succulent that it makes me look down at my hands in wonder—but not until after I spy my perfect shot, lofting at a rate I thought impossible to achieve, a shot I've been searching for all these years, and it's a true beauty. It's not the longest shot, but it comes down and bounces the right way, like a shot you'd see on TV, made by a professional, and all I have is a dinky chip shot to get close to the pin. If the medicine is taking effect, I'll take two, please.

"I'm so scared of those teen years, man," Rhodes says to me. "Nice shot, good work."

I nod my thanks back at him. My spine tingles and the

pain is hurried off by a surge of adrenaline. "Thanks," I reply, holding back the urge to run to Rhodes and throw double high fives at him.

It occurs to me that not only did I apply Rhodes's lesson to my new, more shapely golf swing, but I also might have figured out what Fiona was trying to say to me when she wanted me to be here and not there. I think I did it. I have no idea how, and the subsequent shots over the next few holes are spotty at best because I haven't acquired the knack. But the satisfaction of not reaching so hard and having such grand effects—it's a new sensation. I love golf, even when it slaps me around and takes my hope away. Now Rhodes has given me a dose of something that feels easy and near-magical, and it opens up a new dimension of the game for me.

"Seriously, thank you," I tell him in a moment between moments, somewhere on the eleventh hole. There are three eleventh holes to choose from at Devil's Pulpit. Today, they're using the long par-4. It would be tough to score if you're not striking the ball well. I'm striking the ball well.

"Don't mention it," Rhodes says. "Keep working on it and you'll get good."

"Oh, I'm not saying I'm any good, but now I feel like I have a chance." We share a chuckle. "Hope is all we want, right?"

Rhodes nods. "Hope is all we have."

I jinx myself. I need to attempt my second shot three times. The first time, I hit the ball with the toe of my long iron. It zings so far to the right, I manage to clear a cluster of hills and roll it right into the forest. On the second attempt, I miss the ball entirely: a twisted-up swing-and-miss that brings back the stinger, and I let out an "oh" that prompts Rhodes to ask me if I'm okay. I nod, restart my approach with a sloped right shoulder and neck impingement, and the ball hooks hard and low to the left and down, maybe a hundred yards and directly into the water.

"Good enough," I tell him, and I put the club back into the bag. As we walk to the edge of the water hazard, I think about quitting. I don't need to finish the round, or improve my swing, but I realize I do want to play through the pain if it means I can spend some time with Rhodes, who I'm starting to think could be a friend.

I toss a ball onto the grass near the pond, then take the shot with a 7-iron, my comfort club. I don't prepare. I take the shot, and as I do, my right shoulder fails. It won't move. I cry out, take a knee, and drop the club. My angry nerve endings go from electric-mad to hot as lasers, like a marquee sign of agony. It zaps my ribs for the first time.

Rhodes rushes to me. "What is it?" he says, and I tell him. "We need some ice," is his reply. He gets on his phone and within seconds we see the red beer cart racing toward us. The young woman driving it hops out like a paramedic and runs around to the back to get her supply kit, which is a Safeway bag full of ice cubes from her cooler.

The foursome behind us approach the tees and, spying the scene, hurry down to us as well. I feel like an idiot.

"Can you walk?" Rhodes asks as he starts to guide me to the beer cart, but like James Brown on stage, I refuse to be coddled. I doff the ice pack and head back to my ball.

"We can keep going. It's just pain."

One of the guys behind us shrugs at another, like he's saying, "Can you believe this guy?" I thank everyone for their concern and apologize for slowing the game up. They issue their cordial denials, insisting it wasn't any type of imposition, and the game resumes. The beer cart girl says something to Rhodes. I think she speaks French. It sounds like instructions for the ice bag. She drives off as I twist the club back and grimace as I swing.

I offend the eleventh hole with my horrid golfing, take double-par on my mental scorecard, and we move on.

"You're sure you're okay?" Rhodes asks, and I lie to him.

If the agony of this nerve pinch, or whatever it is, hadn't already taken my breath away, the views of the Niagara Escarpment and far-off Toronto would do it. There is not a single square foot of Devil's Pulpit that is perfectly flat; it's shaped in sweeping curves and cambers that make the place feel like a green spaceship that has landed near Caledon, Ontario. It's a brilliantly crafted layout, although different than a McBroom course. It almost feels like a sculpture. They must have excavated acres of earth to make this course, just dug it right out of the land. If this place feels like a sculpture, a McBroom course would feel like a dance. An evil, impossible dance.

"Hold it close, nice and strong," Rhodes says. "Work at it. Use the big muscles."

How big?

PAR: 72   SCORE: 109

Payne has left his door open a crack.

As I reach for the doorknob, he slams it shut, the force of it enough to bend my hand backward and twist my wrist. I let out a groan of pain and clutch my left hand with my right.

He opens the door and looks at me, steel-faced. He waits for me to say whatever it is I want to say. We've been through this dance so many times that we barely require words for it. He gestures with a single eyebrow hair. I reply with my entire face, every sinew throwing the rage and betrayal back at him. I feel my neck muscles add their two cents. Showing him how much his indifference is killing me sure does make my back hurt.

"Please, can't we be friends again? I hurt you, you hurt me. It's all unintentional." That's what I wish I could say.

"I will take the hinges off this fucking door," is what I say instead.

Payne's eyes go glassy and his eyelids soften. His lips disappear into his mouth like he's found a way to pull himself into himself. He steps backward, then turns and sits on his bed with his laptop so he can move his vacant look to the halcyon glow of the screen.

"Go ahead," he emits, like a wisp from an extinguished candle. "Fuck," he says as punctuation, because I said it, and we had a deal that neither of us would use that kind of language.

"This is not how a son behaves," I tell him as I hold my wrist and try not to bawl.

"Okay, James," he says, and without thinking I burst into his room, rip the laptop off his bed, and throw it into the hallway. It makes a dent in the wall that I'll need to fix later.

I can see myself, being how I'm being, like I'm looking down at myself while perfectly still at the apex of a backswing. I know how awful I've made everything. That wasn't my intent. Now I know I'm capable of being this.

Faith stands by the wreckage of the laptop on the hallway floor. Her first look is to her boy, genuinely afraid for him, never mind whether or not I might be okay.

Clearly, I'm not.

6

NIAKWA, 2011
Manitoba: Eighteen Holes
Stanley Thompson

I am here. This is not a dream. I'm really at Niakwa.
It does *feel* like a dream; as I flip from one desecrated shirt to the next, I've gone directly from Devil's Pulpit to the check-in desk at Niakwa Golf and Country Club, a stone's throw from where I grew up. I always thought someone would call the police if they caught me here. I expected pointed fingers and blue-bloods shouting, "Wrong side of the tracks! He's right there, officer!"

Talk about privilege: when I was young, other kids (from literally the other, better side of the train tracks) were junior members here at Niakwa. I have no idea how much that would cost, but it must have been the equivalent of a used car, probably, which they were each given on their sixteenth birthdays. These were the kids whose parents owned businesses, performed surgeries, or handled the divorces of parents like mine. My mom was a clerk. She raised me and Lane on her own. I had one golf club and used it once in a while at the school grounds while the country club kids got weekly lessons with the pros, then retired to their locker rooms to complain about their awful, tragic lives: "Oh, the car I was given for my sixteenth birthday is a stick-shift! Oh, boohoo!"

And now, here I am.

Who is Rhodes to tell me about privilege? And who am I to talk about tales of woe? I look down to make sure my shirt is tucked in. I have no recollection of putting this outfit on, but it appears to comply with the dress code. I'm dressed in all black, looking as sleek as this middle-aged body can look: sleek like a sea lion. My Niakwa Golf and Country Club logo is on my chest, where it belongs.

There are more exclusive clubs in Winnipeg, like St. Charles, and there are more challenging ones, like the infamous links of Thomas McBroom's Southwood, but Niakwa speaks to me.

I lived next door and pressed my nose against its windows all my life. As I grew to appreciate golf course architects, the fact that Stanley Thompson designed Niakwa simply added to its mystique for me. Back in the 1920s, he churned out a number of the most famous courses in Canada, like the Banff Springs Hotel Golf Course, and Fundy National Park. If you're a golfer in Canada, you have probably played one of his courses. If you haven't, you probably dream of it.

My boss, Karl, is a member at Niakwa, and I suspect that Boreal Building Products pays the membership dues because golf is supposed to be good for business. And it typically is, if you don't FISM your way into a shame-spiral that sours into a pissy mood. You're supposed to laugh it off, display some humility, and let your client feel like the bigger person.

The morning we're supposed to play, he calls me and says he can't make it, but he's called the pro shop and pulled a favour, and I can go anyway. I should bring some-one—he suggests Krista, because Faith doesn't really golf. Not at places like this.

I decide to go on my own.

The curly-haired woman at the podium who scribbles in all the tee times and member names examines me up and down, then hands me the diamond-shaped keychain with a key to a power cart, and then looks down at her book.

"We had to pair you," she says to me. "You're not to take any pictures with your golfing partner, and we very much appreciate if you … are discreet about sharing stories of today. *Ça marche pour toi?* That works?"

I nod, but her strict warning makes me more curious than anything.

I don't even know what she's talking about until World-Famous-Film-Star Scott Branch comes lumbering up to me, a king can of beer in each hand. He hands me one— "for driving around with me today. I'm Scott."

I take the beer and shake his hand. In person, he looks more … chiselled. His bone structure looks more detailed, or sculpted, perhaps. He's shorter than I thought. Clearly he has purchased a new salt-and-pepper hairline, because it's a little too perfect to be real, but flecks of grey have been installed to better match his age. Even Scott Branch is no match for time's corrosive effects, but they didn't need to add any makeup to make Scott Branch look like a stud; it's exactly how he looks in person. Stocky, strong, expressive. Still vibrant. Well-sunned. A movie star. It's a little-known fact that Winnipeg has long been a place for Scott-Branch-types to find some quiet.

I am shaking hands with *the* Scott Branch. "James," I say, weakly.

As he holds my right hand, he points to my left. "Lucky glove?" he asks.

My glove is filthy. The butt of my palm is black from holding the grip so tight. I go through them so quickly, I buy gloves in multiples. Thankfully, I have a brand new one in my bag.

"Listen, they wanted to punt you from your time because this was the only time I could make, but I insisted they let you golf when you were supposed to. I hope this doesn't mess with your round too much, pairing up with me."

I know I am in for a disaster round because the nerves are making me tremble already. Of course I'd never admit it to Scott Branch, and so I shrug it off like it's nothing. No problem. I didn't want to give this course my best anyway.

Scott looks up at the sun, which seems to brighten under his gaze, as though Scott is fuelling it with his eyes. We walk to our cart as other golfers take surreptitious pictures with their phones. I try not to notice.

"Great day," Scott says to me. "I wish everyone could experience four hours like we are about to experience them, James. They call it privilege for a reason."

"Now I feel guilty," I tell him.

"Why? Appreciate what's happening, man. Life isn't equal or fair, nor should it be. Lap up the good stuff and spit out the hot dog water, man!"

I take a big gulp of my beer. I guess Scott's privilege will remain unchecked.

The first four holes go past like a bullet train. It's all I can do to keep the ball on the fairway, and I manage to tame my nerves enough to score not so badly—a bogey on the first, par on the second and third, and another bogey on the fourth. A decent start. Scott plays a typical old man's game: short and straight as an arrow, right up the middle. Nothing fazes him, even after he lands in a bunker and hits the sand wedge straight up into the lip, shooting his ball right into the toe of his shoe.

"I meant to do that," he says, on his way to a triple. After four holes, I am outscoring Scott Branch, and that settles the butterflies down big time. Right now I feel how I imagine Chi-Chi must have felt all the time: rolling. Present in the moment. Communing with the grass.

"My father-in-law was a massive fan of yours," I tell Scott. "He would be amazed to find out this is happening."

The way Scott can put drinks away also reminds me of Chi-Chi.

Niakwa is designed so you can overindulge, quickly if you want to. There is a crossroads that a golfer encounters four times during their round, and at the centre of the crossroads is a well-stocked shack full of alcohol and friendly young staffers encouraging you to buy from them. And that's on a normal day.

Today is not a normal day. We pass the shack after the

fourth hole and the young woman tending bar swoons over Scott. Her phone is out before we even arrive. Scott takes the obligatory selfies, even gets the girl to retake the picture because her eyes weren't completely open in the first shot upon further review. Scott is a nice guy.

He returns to the cart with four shot glasses full of creamy liquor under one hand, two bottles of beer in the other hand, and a half-full two-six of spiced rum nestled in his armpit.

After some juggling, we fill the cup holders with drinks and I thank him profusely.

"You think this is for you?" he says, and I stammer, but he lets me off the hook with a guffaw that outsizes him, nudges me in the ribs with his elbow, and hands me two of the shot glasses.

"China White," he says. "Drink up. We got more drinks than cup holders. Nowhere to put these except down your gullet." He does a father-son-holy-ghost cross with his shooter and then pounds it back.

"Come on," Scott says. "The power of Golf compels you! Drink up."

And so I become inebriated on a glorious sunny afternoon at Niakwa Golf and Country Club with a world-famous movie star, and proceed to get a member's bounce from the right side of the green; straight left and three feet from the hole, an easy putt for birdie. Scott Branch hoots and applauds all the way and I can't help but smile, even as the Earth's axis seems to wobble.

I have no idea what Scott scores on the fifth hole, but as he plucks our golf balls from the cup, I come to a sudden recollection, somewhere from the furthest shelves in the back of my mind, that Scott Branch died a bunch of years ago. Obviously I'm misremembering, because he's right here. Maybe my shit memory is bleeding into my golfing memory? I must be drunk, or maybe I've entered some type of psychotic break where reason yanks its pants down and moons me.

I am doubly suspicious because my golf game has reached a new pinnacle. My body has achieved a Zen-like flow; my clubs are light as divining rods, making the ball squish with each stroke like it's a strawberry wrapped in ionomer resin. This must be what being "in the zone" feels like for an athlete. I have never felt this before.

It's a trick of the memory. It must be. Delusions of grandeur, in reverse.

I remember how Chi-Chi loved Scott Branch movies. In them, Scott was macho and smooth; he could play a cowboy or a spy or any twentieth-century male archetype. He was beloved for it for decades. Scott Branch was a relic of a forgotten time. I think Chi-Chi believed it was probably a better time. He would love to know how affable Scott Branch is—and how they both have the same perfect head of salt-and-pepper hair.

Then my back sends me an extremely unsubtle reminder that I am in the land of the living, for living is pain and I'm definitely experiencing pain. The place where my hip meets my thigh suddenly feels like it's in a vice that twists, to the point where I grimace. I reach into my pocket for my phone. I think to call Faith and ask her for help, or maybe to Google Scott Branch, but my phone isn't there. I remember where I left it: plugged into the damn phone charger that I told Faith was in the wrong spot, because if I don't see it, it doesn't exist, and I knew I would forget my phone and now I have. Another wave of agony whips through me.

"You all right?" Scott asks me. I'm not. I rest my club against my thigh so I can grab my back with both hands and Scott ushers me to the cart and helps me to sit. I tell him it's only a twinge, that it's okay, not a big deal, and even though I can't feel my feet I know it's going to get better, that everything always gets better. This, too.

But it lingers. I lose track of what's happening as the pain makes me turn inward, and I'm back at home for a second, arguing with Faith about that goddamn phone charger and the phone charger is not just the phone charger, and I don't see me in the house at all. I see Faith, and Payne gets the basement, and I've got the garage and my stupid vandalized Hall of Fame, and nothing else. So why should the phone charger be any different? Faith tells me that's exactly what I do every time I'm not in control—I paint everything with this black brush, claiming that everything is terrible, and it yanks the rug right out from under her and Payne both.

Scott is on the phone when I finally snap out of my pain-induced daydreams.

"All set. You're going to be fine, Jimmy-Boy," Scott says to me, like I'm his best bud. "All you gotta do," he gestures to the red flag of the sixth green, "is finish this hole."

I am drunk but it doesn't dull the pain at all. I straighten myself out as much as I can, but I want to know where Faith and Payne went before I ended up in the Hall of Fame. And where they went while I was golfing, when it was all I seemed to be doing, as if I didn't have a career or a family at all. That's how it's felt this last little while, like

I was a perpetual golfing machine. No breaks, no respite: only golf and its endless pursuits.

"Why don't you try to peel your eyes away from that screen for two minutes?" I tell Payne.

Payne doesn't say a thing. He pulls on his hoodie, picks up his tablet, and gets out of his bed like I'm not even there.

"Not going to say anything?"

"I'll have my screen time at Adam's if you're gonna be like that," he says, and I'm scoffing before he even finishes the sentence.

"And how do you plan to do that if you're grounded?"

"I'm not," he says to me. "Talk to the boss."

"Let him go," Faith says from behind me and Payne uses the distraction to slip past us.

"What are you doing?" I ask Faith. "He can't go, he's grounded." The back door slams.

"He needs to get out and do something social. Keeping him locked up will only make it worse." Faith says it with her typical post-Chi-Chi lifelessness, like she doesn't even care. The circles under her eyes make her look like a zombie. Like she hasn't slept for a thousand years.

"We are supposed to be on the same team," I plead with her.

"It's been long enough." We engage in a stare down, and I can't tell her how much I need her to come back and be Faith again. Instead, I follow Payne out the back door and set up the practice net.

A few hours later, I see them drive away from me, and there's nothing else to remember.

My good luck at Niakwa continues. I hit a slicing, fat shot that should advance me twenty yards, but it rifles down a paved cart path, nails an orange OB marker, and kicks left, fifty yards from the green. Scott looks at me and shakes his head.

"I'd ask to borrow your horseshoe but I know where it's been," he says to me. I laugh and everything is easy again. It's easy being Scott. The rest of the hole goes by swimmingly. I score a par. Scott does the same, as though it is a formality we must rush through before we get to his big surprise, lurking at the tee box at the seventh: two portable massage tables, each with a masseuse. Painted dressing screens are set up near the trees so we can change into towels.

"Let's get those lumbars loosey-goosey, Jimmy-Boy."

"You're unbelievable," I say to him.

"Go ahead and play through," Scott barks at a foursome as they catch up to us. We're getting massages in the open air of Niakwa Golf and Country Club, which is completely eccentric and wild and couldn't have been needed more.

"Golf," Scott says. "It gets in your brain. Oh man, that's the spot."

The massage is unbelievable. The masseuse, Lorna, works my back with a combination of precision and brute strength that releases every fibre of strain as she runs along my body's ley lines with her forearm. She's been doing this for years, I'm sure. I let out a moan. Can't be helped.

"Hey, Jimmy-Boy," Scott says cheerfully. "Can I ask you something?"

"Anything, my friend. Anything."

"You ever been ... how do I put this?" His voice trails off.

"Ask me anything," I tell Scott, and I mean it. I am open to him.

"Nah, it's all right," he says. "Forget I said anything."

"What? You can tell me." If he confides in me, then we'll become closer. I'd like that.

"We're having fun here. Don't worry about it."

"Hey, I mean it, Scott. Ask. No bad questions. Least I can do for this. So amazing," I mutter as Lorna releases some kind of aura tingle that rolls through me like a wave of endorphins.

"I get this feeling sometimes, man. Like I'm *truly* alone. You get that?" Scott sighs.

I pull my head out of the donut-shaped cushion it's resting in and offer him a confused look.

Scott clarifies: "Not alone in the usual way—not all by yourself—I mean truly alone."

"Sure, I guess…"

"No, you don't get it. Not really. The only way to feel this alone is to be surrounded by people all the time, man."

"I think maybe I do, Scott. You don't have to be famous to get that kind of feeling."

"Sometimes it's like the real me is somewhere at the bottom of the ocean. You know what I mean?"

Something happens in Scott's eyes when he poses the question. He goes off somewhere, like he's living somewhere else. Of course I know how he feels.

Faith and Payne, in the car together, drive away. I chip the ball into the net. And again. And again. I tell myself this is how I like things. This is what I wanted. To golf, alone.

Another ball makes its way onto the roof.

"Ever feel like that James?" Scott says to me, and I choke

on my words, because it isn't easy to offer counsel to a movie star, especially when you're face-down on parallel massage tables, two-point-nine sheets to the wind.

"We come into the world alone and that's how we leave it, Scott," I manage to say. "Sad truth."

"Most truths tend to be." Scott looks off into the distance. He forces that famous Scott Branch, shit-eating grin back onto his face. "I think maybe I thought I would stop feeling alone if I made friends with the whole world, you know? Turns out that it doesn't work like that. But you know what?" Scott pauses to thank his masseuse as the massage ends and he rolls his towel around his waist. "Maybe this feeling that we're more than our lives, maybe that's what you and I get to share, buddy. We're more than what we do or what we have, right?"

As we get dressed and prepare to re-intoxicate ourselves before embarking on the round, I sense a difference in Scott, like he has been soured by our conversation. His shoulders sag a bit and he walks slowly to the cart with a vacant look on his face, like he has retreated further inside. His eyes are glassy.

As I give Lorna a twenty to thank her for a transformative, surreal massage, Scott pulls the rest of the rum out of the golf cart and pours.

Scott raises his cup and offers a toast: "To being human. Never fully alone, always a little alone. Never truly yourself."

Not knowing what else to add, I raise my cup in reply, say, "To us," and pound it back.

Scott eyes me. "You mean 'you and me' us, or 'all of humankind' us?"

"I guess kind of both." My muscles feel great.

I play the best golf of my life. The scenery improves with each hole. Scott takes pulls of rum straight from the bottle, dispensing with the formality of a plastic cup. It feels self-destructive. I flirt with par on the back nine.

We're at the tenth, having passed the alcohol-stocked shack again, when Scott begins to wobble a bit. He asks me, "You think it's easier or harder to feel alone when everybody thinks they know you?"

"I'm sure it's tougher, Scott." I think he's looking for pity. He's not getting it from me. "So tough. I'm sure your millions of dollars and ability to do whatever you want whenever you want are a sizeable consolation prize. You'll get by. I believe in you."

We are both punch-drunk. Scott has a hard time saying "fuck you" but he manages to spit it out, like a sloweddown vomit. I didn't mean to offend him quite this much, so I apologize. "I'm enjoying all this privilege you have," I tell Scott. "I think you should enjoy it too, man. Being lonely is a friggin' universal human condition." Suddenly I feel like I'm comforting myself.

Faith drives away with Payne. I'm sure they'll be back. Wherever they go, here I am.

In that moment, a realization splits me in half: I haven't been there for Faith after she lost her dad because my heart is a goddamn stone. It hardened up for a good reason, though: you're supposed to lose your father. For me, losing my brother Lane at such a young age, I think that must have hardened me to the goddamn core. The world is full of loss and pain, but however it goes, here I am, and fuck, it's still me.

I need to share this breakthrough with Faith, as soon as possible. Maybe after I sober up a touch.

First, I have to keep golfing. My score is the best it's ever been. This round is like a dream I never want to wake from. Faith and Payne can wait a bit longer.

Scott takes an absent-minded hack at his ball and slices it right, straight into the creek that runs on the right-hand side. He stares at it for a second, leaning forward and back, overcompensating for gravity trying to bring him down.

Instead of playing another ball or walking to the water, he looks as though an idea has struck him and he turns to me.

"What do you think all of this means, Jimmy-Boy?"

"All of what?"

He stretches his arms out like he's presenting the world to me. "This. Golf. The ball. The fuggin' hole at the end. Trying to navigate the world and ending up in the white place, the white fuggin' vortex with a giant flag sticking out of it like it's the top of Mount Everest. Why? What the hell are we doing?"

I look down at my ball and try to think of what I need to do next to get this little dimpled globe into its final resting place in as few strokes as possible. It needs to get past the left edge of the creek and then draw left to roll away from the bunker. I need to focus through the booze if I'm to do this, and I try to visualize my geometry to get the swing path to intersect with the vector laid out by the club face angle. Then it occurs to me, like a message from Gabriel: I am pissed out of my fucking tree.

"Fun, right? It's to have fun?" I say to Scott. "Have fun and make physics bend to our goddamn will. This is the most unnatural thing we can do with nature. Or maybe"— I interrupt myself with a hiccup—"maybe we do this *to* nature. We're a fucking cancer, man."

"Done widdis shit," Scott says. He throws his hands up and then down, like he's discarding all of it. He stumbles back to the cart and plunks down on the seat.

"Hurry up. I'm out of rum," he barks at me, but I don't let it interrupt my stroke. I execute perfectly. It's like I have control over the ball as it travels, making it spin left—but not too left—and I feel like I can see it rotate, that diametrical black line spinning perfectly over and around, and then suddenly it's heading for the hole. Up it goes onto the green, away from the bunker, leaving me with a two-foot putt for birdie.

I can't take my eyes off of it. *I did that.* I can't believe it.

I look over at Scott to see if he was watching how my ball rolled up the green so perfectly, as though I have some kind of telekinesis, but he's looking down at his spikes. "I'm out of rum," he says again, meekly, and then blubbers into his hands, clearly too depressed to get drunk and too drunk to be out here.

I walk over to Scott. "Hey, hey," I offer weakly. I slide into the cart and rest a hand on his back. He cranks the throttle and blubber begets wail.

"I did all of it *wrong*," Scott howls, punctuating the "wrong" like a child in mid-tantrum. "You … you got a family, you got love. That's as good as it gets, man. Good as it gets. What's the sum total of everything I got? Fuck all."

Scott Branch has veered into melodrama. "Come on," I tell him. "Let's get you back to the clubhouse."

"What? No, you gotta finish, Jimmy-Boy. You don't quit. You got lots to fight for, man."

"I got lots to get home to, Scott. Let's both get out of here."

Suddenly, I feel ready to lay down my weapons so I can get the home fires burning. I'm ready to stop being alone.

"Finish up," he says to me. "It's fine. Finish your dream round, son."

I chew my lip for a moment, unsure, but Scott flings an arm in a "get-going" gesture and it prods me to drive to the side of the green. I get out of the cart and study the scene.

Straight in, uphill, two feet. Typically, I would take a gimme from two feet away, but it's for birdie, at Niakwa, and I don't want to look like I'm cheating. I glance at Scott, hoping he'll maybe give it to me, but he looks at his shoes and the weeping lets up for a moment.

"You got this, Jimmy-Boy," he says to me through tears. Nothing more cringeworthy than a sad clown being sad.

I crouch behind the ball, nearly toppling over as I shift my weight. A tiny bit of break but uphill enough to keep my putt on a line, like it was destined to hit the back of the cup and make that sound—that plastic-on-plastic sound that can't be recreated any other way. I stand up and make the shot. That sound. No one has ever named the sound of the ball falling into the cup. It has some tonal similarities to ice falling into the glass of gin and tonic you've been waiting all day to drink. It's the sound of satisfaction.

After ten holes, I'm now four strokes over. I could break eighty! If I break a hundred, I'd be ready to celebrate. This is a round of a lifetime for me.

The thought of breaking eighty is surreal, but I keep my exuberance to myself as much as I can. Sad Scott looks at me with a half-grin mustered onto his face and he says, "Nice" with no conviction at all. "Now, if you don't mind, I need to bury myself in the welcoming bosom of over-priced amber rum." I oblige.

The cart ride to the clubhouse isn't far—the length of the tenth hole—and Scott sniffles as we drive up and down the rolling hills. He gets quizzical looks from the group we pass, who obviously recognize him and clock his tearful countenance. He wipes his face with his forearm and looks away, but the two men say something and smirk coyly. Scott and I both know their comments are not kind.

"Everywhere I go, I'm still fuggin' *me*," Scott says. "Even Wisconsin."

"Winnipeg."

"Winnipeg is what I said."

As we come to a stop, I realize I might just be Scott's best friend in this moment. It took ten holes, and now I'm his caretaker. I can't roll him off of this cart and send him back to his booze and soul-crushing loneliness. But I need to get home too. It's time.

I mean, not before I finish this special round of golf.

Scott can't even sit up straight as he twists back to shake my hand. "Been a pleasure, Winnipeg," he says. "Thanks for the game."

"Thanks for the massage, Scott," I reply. "This has been … memorable. Good to meet you."

"You're a lucky son of a bitch, Jimmy-Boy."

With that, Scott Branch proves that he could never truly know me.

I wait patiently at the eleventh to slot back in. The marshal requires an explanation for why I left the course and then returned, but it's all easily explained away and she seems genuinely pleased that I was kind to their drunken VIP.

I don't want any distractions so I let another pair play through. This way I can attack the course alone. I can attack eighty.

Even though eighty is a score, not the enemy, I have given this number a pair of yellow eyes, dragon's wings, and a set of gnarled fangs. My fairway wood has become Valyrian steel. I am going to slay eighty. And then I'm going to find out what that feels like, and whether I should expect to slay eighty again and again on even more challenging terrain than this, or if I should walk away from golf forever, and maybe by slaying it I will truly understand it. Will I become more of a man? A stronger warrior? More authentically me?

The twelfth proves to be an easy par-3, playable with an 8-iron. I miss a birdie putt by inches, but maintain par. Still four over—seventy-six if I par the rest.

I play a conservative, light drive onto the thirteenth, roll my second onto the edge of the green, lag putt to get close, and then tap in. Four over. Whatever the new elixir is that I've consumed, I welcome it in. I pray it seeps into my cerebrospinal fluid.

The fourteenth is the shortest hole on the course, which is a relief. Less room for error and I get to go home sooner.

I wonder if Faith and Payne are at home right now. Are they angry with me? I can't seem to remember. For this opening shot of about a hundred yards, I employ a gap wedge and leave it a couple of yards short. I roll the chip past the hole and leave myself a tough downhill putt of maybe ten feet. I miss. Bogey. Five over with four holes left.

I've sobered up completely. I want to break eighty more than anything I've ever wanted in my life. I never thought I would ever sniff at this opportunity but I'm now thinking of seventy-seven. PGA golfers hit seventy-sevens. I could play in tournaments if I play this well all the time. But why am I playing this well now?

The fifteenth possesses a narrow fairway, but I manage to stay close to it with my drive. I'm not messing with spin anymore; I'm playing the most conservative game I can play. I need a 9-iron to stick it onto the green, and then my first putt leaves me only a foot away, a single tap and pulled on a string toward the hole. No problem. Par. Plus five. I am out-thinking Stanley Thompson himself.

I get myself to the sixteenth tee and my knees weaken as I stride up to the tee box. Trees crowd me on either side, then open up like a Busby Berkeley synchronized swimming production toward the lake, which is where I will end up if I hit the ball straight or even slightly to the left. The wind blows right-to-left on this par-5, and I'm more than five hundred yards away. A strange thought enters my mind. "*Stop reaching,*" Rhodes said to me during our round. I select a 5-iron for my tee shot and aim to the right side of the fairway. I don't bomb it by any means, but I hit it nearly two hundred yards and it lands in playable grass, a shade inside the first cut. Like a pro, I have avoided the hazard that beckoned and mocked me from the tees. In your face, Stanley! Now I need to take it home.

Another 5-iron gets me about sixty yards away. I mess up the lob wedge and hit it on the bounce—the bottom part of the club head where the letter L is engraved. But the result works in my favour. The ball travels on a low trajectory, up the green to its topmost edge. I have two putts to make it, so I try to get within three feet on my first putt. I leave it light and I've got a six-foot putt, downhill with a sharp right break.

This course is immaculate and I feel grateful for that, for its predictability but also its beauty, and I take a moment to revere nature and its physical assets. The lands upon which we traverse are as holy as we are, as divine as the shining white globe we advance with our best intent. Whoever cares for this course also loves it; of that I am certain. I blow the second putt past the cup. My third putt from three feet away rings around the lip before finally draining, and I am not angry about it at all. Plus six. Two holes remain. I have only one stroke to give back to par if I'm going to slay eighty. I tell my putter to be ready as I return it to its sheath.

A fairway bunker on the seventeenth collects my tee shot, and my heart along with it.

I cruise up to it in my power cart, every bump feeling like a taunting kick to the shins. I consider cheating. I realize I haven't taken a single mulligan or kick, which is unusual for me, or any other golfer I know, except Chi-Chi.

"The best part of golf," Chi-Chi had said, *"is that you can cheat as much or as little as you want."*

I decide to keep the round clean and virtuous. I feel like I'm on a pilgrimage and I let that feeling guide me as I stand at the precipice of this bunker, my ball a good three feet below, mired in thick, cream-coloured sand. The same thickness as the sand at Victoria Beach.

It's hard to convey the impression one gets when they are tucked into a cottage at Victoria Beach with their closest family members; it's like you've stepped into a painting of a quaint village planted on a peninsula with an inland ocean surrounding you on three sides, the arms of Lake Winnipeg embracing the land like a prehistoric hug. Victoria Beach holds you like a familial embrace. This place is a comfort.

Victoria Beach is the largest jurisdiction in the Western Hemisphere that forbids motor vehicles on its roads during the tourist season. From June until October, everyone walks or rides a bike, and the bikes you see are typically ancient cruisers that have enjoyed more Manitoba summers at the beach than the people who ride them.

Some things have changed. The beaches have eroded away, leaving only a sliver of the play area I enjoyed with my brother and beach friends when I was young. Even Payne noticed the changes once he managed to unglue his retinas from the screen of whatever device he brought to the beach; one year the algae would be thick as sludge and toxic blue; another year, the zebra mussels would pile up like sunflower seed shells. Vans patrol the dirt roads now, an exception to the vehicle restrictions, either to ferry the infirm and their luggage to and from the massive parking lot, or to run security checks on the million-dollar Sunset Boulevard mansions that masquerade as cottages. For me,

Victoria Beach will always be a safe, secluded place for a family to act like a family, in spite of all the change. When it's my turn to kick the bucket, and my life does the final run-through that people say it's supposed to do, the final frame I want to see will be this:

Sunset with my camera in my hand, snapping photos of Faith and Payne while they walk through the sand, twisting their feet with each step, a summer dance that propels them through this paradise; they are bathed in light from the crimson sunset, which paints shadows into each sandy foot-step they leave behind. Faith's red hoodie matches Payne's bathing suit. I kneel in genuflection, taking picture after picture, moved to the verge of tears by the beauty of this moment, nearly divine.

This is what life is. This.

"Idyllic" is a word that comes to mind when I think of Victoria Beach. Play. Togetherness. Safety. The golf is an added bonus.

Niakwa Golf and Country Club doesn't smell like Victoria Beach, but I feel like golfing cannot be better than it is in this moment, right now. And if this is the best golf has to offer, then perhaps it is time to get home and try to find that Victoria Beach feeling with my family again.

I swipe at the ball in the bunker and a geyser of sand spews as high as my nose. Somewhere in that mess, my ball has lofted up, but I can't see it in the air. The sand blows back into my nose and eyes, forcing me to turn away. As I stumble out of the bunker, I wipe the guck out of my face and reach for the rake to clean up my footprints. I'm not sure I even want to know where my shot ended up. All I know is that it isn't in the beach anymore.

I put the rake back down, gather my courage, say "okay" to myself, and look out, scanning for the white of my ball in amongst the grass.

I don't see anything on the fairway, so I scan the rough. Nothing.

Oh. Easy enough to spot—it's on the green. I laugh at my good fortune, take two cautious putts, and bring my six-over-par to the final hole, a par-4 that brings you right to the patio where club members can watch you finish your round.

A par would give me seventy-eight. A bogey, seventy-nine. All I need to do is play cautiously and finish my dream round. Then I'll be able to find Faith and tell her we can forget about our problems; that we can let the memories go. I'll bring her into my arms again, closing our distance. I can tousle the chestnut hair of my boy, who will always be my boy no matter how old and funky-smelling he gets, no matter how much he resents my existence. I'll get close to him too. Just as soon as I finish my round of a lifetime and finally get this ball to do what I want it to.

SCORE: 81

The pizza is barely cooked. The crust is limp, the cheese unmelted. We eat it anyway, in front of the streaming TV.

It's winter and I haven't touched a golf club in months. There is no retreat from this winter. Darkness beams in through the window, refracting into our living room. We stare at the new big screen on the wall, a big, rectangular pill for us to swallow, and the programming streams at us faster than we can retain it. We can't even remember what we're watching as we're watching it, but we let the stream wash over us like a satanic baptism.

Payne enters the room and sits down in the rocking chair to join us in our silent streaming.

Faith's face is so pale. The circles under her eyes have become blackjacks, thick with the fatigue of years; a vast tract of her inner world clear-cut when Chi-Chi died. She sits there, electric blanket covering her legs, our cat nestled between them. Faith's got no fight. Her arms rest at her sides, hands open. She lets the programming stream right into her, trying to let go of memory.

I slip my fingers into her hand and she responds in kind. As I tighten, she tightens, and even though life is a nightmare and the years punish us with pain, I feel her and she feels me, and we let the programming wash over us. A tear leaks from the corner of my eye, relieving some pressure.

Someday it will be spring, *I think.* Always know that things will grow green again, on the course and in ourselves, and when it's time to lay out your intention on this sphere, you better know what you're trying to do.

For today, we are all three of us able to watch the same show. If Payne likes it, he'll go downstairs and binge the rest of the series before Faith and I can even get around to the next episode. It's like we've met at a special crossroads in our lives, like concentric orbits that have aligned under this baptizing flood of artificial light. Perhaps we will be reborn.

"Your dad is dead, Faith," I want to tell her. "When do we get to live again?"

Maybe after this, Payne will play one of his video games. Go sulk. Masturbate. Whatever he does, he'll do it alone.

But for right now, we sit in silence, all three of us allowing the stream to wash over us, together. The pizza is awful. We don't pay it any mind.

A secret, mindful wish bubbles up as I try to mindlessly eat and watch the stream: I wish I knew how to get us out of this.

If I'm stuck in the bunker, I select the appropriate club and knock the shit out of the problem. Even if I end up in the rough, at least I know I'm getting somewhere. I can do something. Nothing I do will get us out of this winter.

7

ULUKHAKTOK (HOLMAN), 2009
Northwest Territories: Nine Holes
Billy Joss

I'm remembering that wrong. Billy Joss didn't design this course; it was a group of community members, I believe the locals told me. But Billy Joss is the godfather of golf in Ulukhaktok, formerly known as Holman. He brought golf here. They named their tournament after him: the Billy Joss Open.

I have to admit, the jacket I have from the Billy Joss Open isn't the fanciest, and I don't know if it would even comply with dress codes on golf courses south of 60°, but it keeps me warm. At least it did until the logo on the back got cut out of it.

Legend has it that Billy Joss brought clubs to Holman straight from Scotland, and that he had become so adept with them that he could put a matchstick in the tundra and set it alight with his 5-iron.

Billy was a company man, not unlike me. The Hudson's Bay Company had sent him to Holman to run the Northern Store, but Walter and Myrle, my golf buddies for the day, tell me Billy Joss's real job was to teach the kids in Holman how to golf. And it didn't take long for the game to catch on; the open terrain and dusty tundra surface lends itself well to hitting a few balls. Walter tells me they had a three-hole golf course for many years, with artificial turf greens. If you didn't care for your lie, you didn't have to play it from there; you could carry a turf mat around with you and place the ball on that.

Now I remember: four of the townsfolk developed the six extra holes needed to make it a proper nine, and soon afterward the Open was established, lasting three days and nights the third weekend of every July, during Ulukhaktok's three months of midnight sun. Celebrities would come, like former Edmonton Oilers or ITV newscasters.

Nowadays, the kids in Ulukhaktok play as much hockey as they do golf, but before the rink got built it was all golf, all the time. Half the town played the game by the time Billy passed away, and not only during the three months of thaw; locals found a way to find those golf balls in the snow. Creative ball markings help. Of course, if a raven snatches your ball, you drop a new one with no penalty. You play around the muskox.

I'm on the western shores of the Beaufort Sea, well north of the Arctic Circle, on the coast of Victoria Island. We're a thousand miles north of Yellowknife. I've never been so far away from home. The light is almost indescribable up here. The sun is constant, but so distant, like a lost soul haunting you. The sky is the lightest blue you'll ever see, and the rays of the sun are nearly white, blanching everything.

As a lumber salesman, one notices the distinct lack of trees up here. It must have made Karl salivate when the cooperative that does all the construction projects in Ulukhaktok came calling for a big order. "You want to build a new hockey rink? Sure, I'm overjoyed to become a title sponsor of the Billy Joss Open." Not that Karl would dream of coming up here to participate in it himself, of course. Ulukhaktok ain't exactly Bermuda. It's unlike anything I have experienced in my life. The tournament feels like a community gathering. Outdoor grills sizzle up seal meat and chicken, and giant pots of stew steam into the sky. There's laughter and dancing. People whizz about on their ATVs, dodging muddy dirty-pants children who chase each other all around the course. The tundra leaves its mark on everything, washing us all in earth. We aren't dirty. We're part of it and it's part of us. Those kids are just closer to earth.

I'm paired up with two locals, both in their seventies. Myrle introduces herself and says, "This is my brother, Walter." Walter absently nods at me, but never looks me in the eye. He says something to Myrle in Inuinnaqtun, and then stalks off, swinging his ancient wooden driver in one hand like a scythe.

They seem nice enough, although they mostly speak quietly to each other in Inuinnaqtun. We walk past an unvarnished wood sign with an image of a person in a traditional Inuit parka swinging a golf club. The words etched above the image read: "Welcome to the World's Most Northernly 9 Hole Golf Course In The World."

It's a balmy twelve degrees during the daytime. Golfers typically wear jeans and sweaters or jackets; thankfully, they've given me a black bomber jacket as an honoured guest. Otherwise I would have froze.

I'm trying to see the hole that now lives in my jacket. But right now, I'm in Ulukhaktok. Try as one does, you can't see an absence. You can only see its edges.

Myrle tells me the people used to follow the food, travelling all around the area, but when the Europeans came, they settled everything down. I look at the town site, which is maybe a kilometre from the golf course. It's got a big hockey rink, a couple of churches, a hotel, and a store. It's an outpost, where four hundred people live and golf and try to figure out how to make it work.

"Our tee time is one-thirty-five," Myrle says as she reads from a clipboard.

I look at my watch. Three o'clock. *How did my glove get so filthy already?*

"Wait, we missed our tee time?"

Myrle and Walter look at each other, mutter something I can't make out, and then giggle.

"It's Mountain Time here, right? Same as Alberta?" I ask them. "Isn't it three already?"

"One-thirty-five in the morning, guy," Walter says. "You can slow down."

"When do we sleep?" I ask them, and they both laugh.

"We can do the putting competition while we wait." Myrle says something to him, words in Inuinnaqtun bordering the words "longest drive."

"The longest drive competition too," Walter replies.

I don't remember the long afternoon and evening before our tee time. A lot of it involves sitting, alone and quiet, on a yellow vinyl lawn chair. I watch the local kids hit golf balls and run around. I eat something fatty and peppery that gives me gas. I think it's maybe whale, but no one confirms it. It's good with a Coke. Anytime I start to nod off, an ATV buzzes past and startles me upright. Time becomes a wavy line. I think of home often.

Walter and Myrle take turns paying me a visit every couple of hours. Walter tells me the blade of his putter reminds him of an ulu, a moon-shaped blade not unlike an Italian mezzaluna, except strong and thick and more versatile. Walter tells me that the town's name—*Ulukhaktok*—means "the place where good ulu parts are found."

Finally, Myrle announces that the longest drive competition is about to start, and as I stand up to stretch, she examines my clubs. "Real nice," she says, and I thank her, but she shakes her head and says, "Too nice. You'll wreck 'em." I didn't even consider that. My new clubs are going to be permanently marked up by the loose stones atop the tundra. For a split second, I consider borrowing someone else's clubs. But I know I'll be swinging my own driver. I think a part of me wants my clubs to be marked by this place.

The recreation director is a curly-haired woman with a French accent: obviously a transplant. No one seems to look at her warmly. She's got a personal PA system secured to her waist by a black nylon belt. She speaks to everyone through her CB handset, but it crackles so much that we can't make out much of what she's saying. I hear two words resembling "James Khoury" crackle through the speaker and there is polite applause, so I grab my driver and shuffle my way through the onlookers. They're crowded around a patch of open tundra, with a rolling hill maybe three hundred yards away.

I try to run through my checklist of long drive mechanics: leftward spin, get the backswing up higher and then drop the club head to ensure an inside-out swing, pull down that lead shoulder, and stick that right-hand chicken wing into the rib cage so it doesn't cackle off into the air and turn this into a baseball swing. Legwork ... legwork ... left knee down and then left side up, turn that right hip at the target.

Yes.

A great practice swing.

"Hit the ball next time," a kid shouts from the crowd, and every single person laughs.

"Just warming up," I tell them. I spray the words into the dusty yellow air, trying to strafe the whole crowd.

I rush my swing and the ball, marked with a long, barbell-shaped radial line, shoots off hard to the left. A hook. I've come at it too low after a hacking up-and-down backswing, and there's a collective gasp from the onlookers. If the ball travels a hundred and fifty yards, I'll be pleasantly surprised. There's polite applause, and then Walter's name crackles through the PA. He hits one straight up in the air that outdistances me by fifty yards. Some kid ends up winning first place. He earns himself a dot-matrix-printed certificate of achievement and a handshake from the celebrity handing out the awards: a stand-up comedian that everyone knows from Radio One Inuvik who came all the way down from Tuk.

Time gets wavy again. After some hours, I'm invited to the putting competition, which takes place on a brown green: it's smoothened tundra that behaves almost like the top of a sandbox. My ball leaves a trail behind it in the brown as it travels. I have neither the hope of reading the break, nor the resistance of the dirt against my ball. Add the pressure of putting in front of sixty or seventy people and my attempt is a massive failure. The flatstick carves my ball off of the ground like an ulu separates skin from bone, and after a hop resembling a floundering seal, the putt finishes probably ten feet from the cup and four feet to the right. There are ball trails criss-crossing all over this brown tundra green; no one's putt has traveled where mine has.

From what I recall, the evening feels like morning and all of it blends together. One-thirty in the morning startles me to life and suddenly, after an eternity, it's my turn to play the course.

I play soldier golf from the jump: left, right, left, right, left. It's ugly.

But the golf isn't what I remember or relish from my round at the Billy Joss Open in the middle of a July night in Ulukhaktok. The game is slow, the holes much longer and more challenging than I expected. Even if I played well, the course would be a challenge. Par is an incredible score here, and Myrle tells me that the winner will probably shoot around five-over-par forty.

Walter and Myrle don't play with a lot of joy. They bicker with each other in Inuinnaqtun the whole time. I have no idea what they're saying, but I recognize the rhythm of their back-and-forth. There are a few more syllables per bicker, but it's unmistakeable to me. It's the bickering you can only have between siblings. You can piss them off all you want, be as unpleasant to them as they are with you, and yet quickly forgive and forget.

How I long to have that again.

Walter and Myrle remind me of me and Lane.

"You got a brother?" Myrle asks me.

I nod, but then recant, "Used to."

"Him and me, we forgot how to be nice to each other," she says. "We're too close together."

"Me and my brother, we lived together when we first moved out," I tell her. "I get it. You get so close sometimes, it's like they're inside you."

She looks at me. "When you let a person inside, sometimes they're not gonna like what they find, eh?"

I nod. Her wizened smile is missing an eye tooth. There's an arctic hardness in it.

Each artificial-turf green is surrounded by a moat of stones, presumably to mask the seam of the carpet, but maybe to prevent players from rolling the ball right up onto the green. On the sixth, Walter hits the rocky circle and his ball bounds off to the right. Myrle and I both play decent approaches onto the green, leaving Walter to chip on. He leaves the chip short and in his cursing—all done in Inuinnaqtun—I swear to God I hear the word "FISM." It stops me cold.

"Hey, Walter," I point my putter at him, "did you just say FISM?"

"It's still me, is it not?" he says, looking peeved, then mutters something I can't make out.

Myrle shoots something back in Inuinnaqtun and then turns to me.

"Hey, don't let anybody in who isn't supposed to be in," she says. I think she says that. I'm having trouble knowing. Am I remembering this right?

We play well, but none of us win anything. Despite being on an open plain of tundra with greens made of vinyl turf, you need to know Holman Golf Course to play it well. Like most things in life.

As an honoured guest, I get to keep the jacket. I sleep in it on the flight home.

I come home with one golf ball left in my bag, my clubs covered in dust. My driver is scuffed from the loose tundra silt and my last golf glove is blackened and browned with the beginnings of a hole on the tip of the ring finger.

Every time I leave Faith, I'm relieved. Every time I come home, I'm relieved too. I remember that.

I remember asking Karl if Krista could come up to the Billy Joss Open with me, to represent the company.

I should remember something else.

PAR: 35   SCORE: 53

The last time I golf with Chi-Chi, I play one of my best rounds, and he plays one of his worst.

As he drives us home in his orange pickup truck, I tally up our scores.

"What'd you shoot?" he asks me.

"One-oh-six," I tell him. "And you shot ... one-oh-six."

Chi-Chi cringes. "Jeez. Not great." He has the type of skin you get from spending the whole summer outside for seventy years; his cheek only bears wrinkles when he frowns or scowls, and he only frowns or scowls about twice a year.

"Your one-oh-six is an honest one-oh-six," I tell him in an attempt to comfort. Chi-Chi doesn't do mulligans. He would only offer a gimme putt to someone else and would never accept one for himself. So my score is much more loosey-goosey than Chi-Chi's, always. That's how much more of a man he is than me.

As we pass into Kenora and the truck slows down, Chi-Chi says to me, "Think I'm getting a membership at Beauty Bay next year."

"Is that right?"

"Yep. Golf every day next summer."

That takes me by surprise. "You finally retiring?"

"Semi-retirement. Next spring, I figure."

Faith and her mom, Dorothy, will be thrilled to hear the news. I wonder if Chi-Chi has even told Dorothy yet, or if I'm the lucky one to know this first.

"Yeah, spring, I figure. I'm giving the company six months to plan how to live without me," Chi-Chi says with a hint of that smile of his; the one that starts with a brightness in his eye and then trails down to his lip. He side-glances at me.

"I've seen a lot of guys retire," I say to him. "I think it's like a tour in Vietnam. When you're short and close to your discharge, you need to keep your head down because that's when the stray bullets find you." How the hell do I know anything about a tour in Vietnam? Yet I tell him like I've experienced it first-hand.

He smiles some more; maybe he ponders what I told him as he drives us home.

But Chi-Chi doesn't listen to me. He doesn't keep his head down. No one has any time to plan what we'll do without him.

Staring up into the ceiling, Faith and I attempt a conjugal visit with sleep. Our legs don't touch. We've formed an escarpment of blanket between us. Sometimes we don't kiss goodnight. This is one of those times. It feels like a knife was left in my belly.

"I changed my mind," I tell her.

"About what?" she murmurs, pretending to be more asleep than she is.

"I used to say I hope I die first."

The word "die" makes her pause for a long time. "Yeah," she finally says, unsteadily.

"So I don't have to deal with all of it." I don't say "again," but I mean again.

"Yeah."

"I changed my mind."

Faith lets her silence harangue me. Selfish asshole. What kind of a thing is that to say when your wife is suffering so badly? I hear her harangue me, loud and clear.

She rolls over, farther away, pulling the blankets from me.

But we both know it's true. Her time needs to come before mine.

I remember how I dealt with Lane. I'll never forget how she's dealing with Chi-Chi.

"I mean, I thought I knew how people deal with this type of situation."

"Situation?"

"Poor choice of words."

"Because of Lane?" she says into her pillow. There's a sniffle.

"Because of Lane. Yeah. But I'm so wrong. It's got to be you."

She can't go through all of this ever again.

All she does before we fall asleep is sniffle. I presume her tears wet her pillow again, streaming out of her for reasons she will probably never explain to me.

She probably shouldn't have to.

8

SERENITY, 2019
Alberta: Thirty-Six Holes
Gary Browning

I don't remember touching this particular golf shirt in my Hall of Fame. In my mind, I'm travelling without pause from the overnight round at Ulukhaktok with Walter and Myrle, through dreams of life at home, to a barely familiar course where the Rocky Mountains frame the horizon like jagged teeth. I can see the Calgary Tower from the parking lot.

No, that isn't right. Serenity is some distance from Calgary. I shouldn't be able to see downtown, but I do. And both of the courses here at Serenity are open: Dancing Bull and Sun Catcher. Part of me knows that doesn't jibe with reality. Sun Catcher was a giant mound of dug-up soil still being formed into berms and treachery when I golfed Serenity. Today it's teeming with golfers. That makes me afraid. I elect to golf the course that's familiar in my memory ... landscape I can trust: Dancing Bull.

I'm starting to realize that I can't trust my memory. Faith was right. There's something wrong with me.

When something is wrong with your hand, or your skin, or a muscle in your back, there is distance. These places are connected to you, but still some distance from your core.

When there is something wrong with how you hear, taste, smell ... that is closer to the pin of self, I'd say. When you realize something is wrong with your awareness, you've hit the flagstick. It sends vibrations throughout. It can't be closer to the hole without going all the way in.

I need to find a way to make sense of everything I'm experiencing, this dizzying sequence of memory and dream, and the persistent tugging at the back of my consciousness.

And then, as though in answer to a question I hadn't yet asked, I look off into the distance, past the first green, and see a bull moose staring back at me.

There's no mistaking the silhouette of it. It's frozen in place, staring back at me, perhaps as startled as I am.

Then again, perhaps not, because I suddenly remember that the animal is actually a statue named Monty, placed there by the designer of the course to pay homage to an actual bull moose he saw traversing the landscape before there was a golf course here. Before the designer bent nature to his will, this land belonged to the bull moose. It's a kind gesture for Browning and the course owners to pay homage to this natural heritage.

I should have remembered that. I know I've played here but I can't remember the circumstances. It's an absence that echoes, like when you know you've met someone before but can't place the face. It's there for a flash, and then gone.

My ball is teed up, the same one I used in Ulukhaktok and at Niakwa in Winnipeg: a single line up the middle. The driver I'm holding still bears the dust and scratches of the tundra. My golf glove has a hole starting on the ring finger. The bag is nicked up and dusty from the Billy Joss Open. I know that can't be right, but I see it.

This doesn't feel like memory anymore. I'm going from course to course without pause or interlude, ferried by some unseen force. I'm not selling forest products. I'm not seeing my shirts and reminiscing. I'm either way inside my own head or way outside of it. Either way, this isn't reality anymore. It's golf.

The crisp, cool air of the foothills mixes with the faint smell of dung and cow slaughter wafting in from Brooks. It cauterizes my nostrils. There's no doubt in my mind that I'm actually here. Here, but not here. Standing at the first tee with a driver in my hand and a ball settled on the white wooden pedestal, awaiting my intention. Inert, but ready.

I love to golf, right? It's some kind of metaphor that keeps me going. That's what I like to think.

So I golf.

I grip and rip. The ball flies as though still bound by the physical laws of nature, and so I continue to believe in those laws. The shot lands on the fairway but rolls into a low-lying depression to the right. I pull my clubs, which now sit strapped to a metal pull cart. After about ten strides down the fairway, the soreness returns, growing a spiky tail and sharpening its fangs at the base of my neck. By the time I reach the vicinity of my second shot, the monster is flying up and down my shoulder nerve and breathing fire.

My ball is nowhere to be found, and I am totally cool with it.

I turn around to leave. There is no one else on this course. No one is marshalling. No one is ahead or behind me. There's not another soul.

In fact, there's no road out of here. From the first tee box, I walk back to the corral of power carts and look left, to where I know there should be a road leading away from the golf course. But there is no escape from Serenity.

I rub my neck and stare out at the horizon, trying to figure out what to do. But really, there's only one thing *to* do.

Upgrade.

The keys are in the power carts. I slide my bag into the back of the first one and head back out.

I didn't even see the ball land, but I'm convinced it's a non-issue, even though it was the last ball in my bag. Because I know that if the Forces That Be want me to keep golfing, they're not going to let me lose the ball.

As I approach the tee box to the second hole, which is off to the right of the first fairway, I spot a ball. I'm certain it's mine as I get closer, but after I pick it up and inspect, I'm surprised to find it's not. It's a good ball; one of those five-dollar tour-level balls. The marking is three blue dots in a triangle. "Therefore." A logical conclusion. I appreciate the irony as I arrive at my own logical conclusion: since I lost my ball and there's nobody around to claim this one, I might as well play it.

I drop my found ball about a hundred and sixty yards

from the first green, which sits in front of Monty, the bull moose. I waggle and look up at my target.

Behind it, the moose moves.

Or rather, I see movement around the moose. I stop and stare—was that a leg I saw? I watch Monty for a minute or two, but he's not budging. My mind must be coming up with more tricks.

I hit this second shot so well, it lofts up like an airplane. I can hear the ball's spin cutting through the air with a fizz. It's a beauty of a shot and I hold my follow-through in a perfect position while I watch the ball fly, fly, fly. It's so majestic. It's fifty yards past the green, toward the eleventh hole, where it lands at the feet of a man whose silhouette seems to emerge from the moose statue.

The figure leans against Monty's leg like it's a lamppost on a New York street at night and he's waiting on a friend. The closer I get, the more detail I can make out: this man isn't a day older than twenty-five. The clothes he's wearing would barely pass the dress code for mini-golf, let alone Serenity: baggy jeans and a plaid flannel shirt tied around the waist, like Eddie Vedder. His T-shirt has a hole in its side and says "Ren and Stimpy" on the front.

Perhaps it's my subconscious distracting me from his face. Or maybe the nineties-era grunge garb was enough to do it. Either way, when I finally clock the narrow angle of his jaw, the collection of freckles in a pattern I could draw from memory, the thick mop of dark brown hair that made him look like *Friends*'s Joey Tribbiani circa 1995, I nearly fall to the grass.

My dead brother opens his arms and I fall into them. I wail into his shoulder. I'm not thinking about the how or why. Lane is here. My face touches his shoulder and I am carved open like a rift in the ocean floor. Lane has about a two-inch height advantage on me, still, and the comfort of his arms around me—even his *smell*—overcomes me. The ocean releases its ancient magma of emotions and I'm determined that I never want to leave him again.

"Lane," is all I can croak into his shoulder.

He slides back a bit, gently pushing me away from him. There's a code among brothers, and I'm definitely violating it. You don't bawl like a baby around your brother, even if they've died and you're reunited with them after more than twenty years. There's no crying, no matter how impossibly hard things may get. It's a stupid code.

I look up into his eyes and notice that they look a bit glassy too. "We should get playing," he says. "Don't want to hold things up."

I get to play a round with Lane, I think, and I silently thank the Wizard of Oz, or the Golf Gods, or whoever/whatever is responsible for this. My imagination, maybe.

I wipe my nose and drop the ball on the fairway.

"Grunge golf is so over, Lane."

"Nice pleated golf pants, Arnie."

"Shut the fuck up."

"You shut the fuck up." I want to throw this golf club into the trees and hug him for the rest of my life. "Start golfing, dummy," he says to me and so I put my head down.

My mind fills with so many questions as I pretend to ready my shot:

1. *Are you a spirit trapped in golf purgatory who needs to cross over?*
2. *Can you see my life with some kind of otherworldly bird's-eye view?*
3. *Do you know anything about Faith and Payne?*
4. *Do you think I did okay with my life?*
5. *Did you foresee "paunchy, balding tree salesman" in my future?*
6. *Can you see how bad things got?*
7. *Do you think it's my fault?*
8. *Have you been like this for the past twenty years?*
9. *Am I a golfing ghost whisperer now?*
10. *You think you can still beat me at golf?*
11. *If you were alive, would we golf together?*
12. *Why did you leave us?*
13. *Why did you leave me?*

"Care to make this round interesting?" I say to him as I waggle.

"It wouldn't be golf without a little juice on it," Lane says. "What are the stakes?"

You win, I go with you. I win, you come with me. "Skins," I say instead. "Hundred a hole."

"Oh, big lumber baron is rich now," he says. "I can't cover that." Lane could never cover anything. His mouth wrote cheques all the time, and typically the cheques bounced before they got to your wallet. At least he's being honest about it, now that he's a ghost.

"How about this," Lane says as he examines my clubs in

the cart bag. "We play skins, but every skin is worth one question. Like truth or dare. That way we don't wreck the whole round with chitty-chat. I'm here to golf, Jimbo."

I look at him and paint a cocky smirk onto my face, replete with raised eyebrow, to match the smirk he's giving me. "You're gonna be singing like Mitsou."

"Aww shit, the trash talk begins!" he exalts and I make my shot. It's a perfect pitch shot, hitting the fringe and rolling to the green.

"This hole doesn't count," Lane says after he sees the shot, and I'm brought back into the old dynamic of trying to reason with my little brother. *Typical Lane.*

"Why the hell not?"

"Warm-up hole. I mean, I haven't swung a club in how long?"

I have to concede that point.

"So, there's no way you can take the skin fair and square," he continues. "I'll get limbered up on one and then we start the skins on two. Only fair."

To you, maybe. He withdraws a long iron from my golf bag—he doesn't have his own clubs. He rifles around some more.

"Toss me a ball," Lane says. I give him an apologetic look and gesture to my ball on the fairway.

"It's my only one," I tell him. Lane spins around, hands in his hair, demonstrating that we're at an impasse as dramatically as Lane demonstrates everything.

He glances at the ground between his feet. "Oh, here's one," he says and bends to pick up a fluorescent yellow ball that looks brand new, like it was made for him. "It'll do." He tosses it into the middle of the long grass, grabs my fairway wood, and, without aiming or taking a single warm-up shot, launches it low and straight. The ball comes to a rest about ten feet shy of my own shot.

Lane shrugs and taps the grass down with his toe. I sit down in the power cart. A rush of adrenaline cascades through my body, causing me to shudder, and I feel a wave of cold sweat coming on. My little brother is about to sit down beside me. *My little brother I thought I would never see again.*

He looks into the distance. I can't take my eyes off of him. He was always trimmer than me, with a more sculpted jaw and squarer features, and that hasn't changed. Since I've aged since 1999 and he hasn't, the differences are even more pronounced than they already were.

In 1999, Lane went to Australia and never came back.

Lane had planned to do a one-year sabbatical Down Under, to avoid the big, frightening world of responsibility that almost had him cornered: he was a week from graduating his computer engineering program when something spooked him. He had completed a couple weeks of internships with two different firms; Lane told me he did well and was expecting offers from each business once he graduated. Maybe that's what spooked him. Or maybe he was trying to get away from a romantic entanglement that he had kept private. Maybe it was living with me. He never told me. All I knew was that suddenly he was gone, bumming around Australia with a friend, and when the friend came home after a month, Lane announced he was staying for as long as his visa would let him.

Bondi Beach got too expensive, and so he moved to a suburb on the outskirts of Sydney with a work buddy, a guy named Arun who was also on a temporary work visa but had planned his year properly. Talking on the phone then got too expensive too, and so our phone calls went from one every two weeks to one a month, and email was only useful if Lane could get to an internet café and access his account. That happened about once a month also. By the time we found out he was about to die, it was too late to get on a plane to see or help him. He was going to die from whatever virus had laid him up for the previous two weeks, and thankfully he was lucid long enough to phone us or we would never had known at all.

According to his roommate Arun, Lane started to feel like he had the flu and tried to power through it, partying and working and being Lane. He had a virus, but it wasn't the flu. The day his temperature spiked to 104°F and he could barely breathe because his lungs were so full of fluid, Lane insisted Arun not call us. Lane didn't want to worry us and he knew our mom wouldn't be able to sleep or eat if she found out.

The whole family lived in terrified silence and darkness for endless days, not knowing what was killing Lane or how we could help. And then he died. His life ended and my life would never be the same.

Lane died of what turned out to be West Nile virus, but we didn't know it at the time. Our dad couldn't be away from his motorcycle business for more than a day, so it was Mom and me who went to Australia to pick up his body. Mom identified it, because somebody had to, and I couldn't. I would rather never see Lane again than see his lifeless face, because Lane's face had the most life in it of any face.

Sitting here, now, right beside me, he looks and smells

and is exactly how I remember him in 1999 when he left for Australia.

I have no desire to awaken from this dream.

The rules of a skins game are simple: each hole is worth a skin and one golfer wins it by shooting a lower score that his opponents. If no golfer wins the hole by scoring in fewer strokes than his competitors, then the skin is added to the next hole. Skins make for good gambling: a skin can be worth a fixed dollar amount, or an amount that increases as the round goes on. I think of how my questions might increase in relevance as we get closer to the end, but there's no way I can hold back. I need to know about everything Lane has experienced in the lifetime since I last saw him, and I need to know right away. Has it only been the blink of an eye for Lane?

We finish off the first hole with little fanfare. I catch his eye a couple of times and look so deeply into them that it makes us both uncomfortable. I want desperately to ask him if he is okay, if he is happy, if there's a way we can stay together after this round of golf is over.

What if this round of golf never ends? I have so many questions.

"What?" Lane says to me as he readies his tee shot on the second hole. "You got a weird look on your mug, like you're scheming up an evil plot."

"Lane, you know you're dead, right?"

"That's a question, Jimbo. You haven't won the skin yet." He smashes his tee shot low, off the bottom of the club head, and his yellow ball barely gets six feet above the ground. The drive goes a hundred yards at most.

If I golf the way I've been golfing the last couple of

rounds, I could win this hole and get my questions answered. On the other hand, if I drag the game out by playing terrible golf then I'll get even more time with Lane, and that's worth more to me than any number of questions I could ask him. Plus, if I lose the only golf ball I have, who knows how much time that could buy me? I decide to switch tactics.

Lane hands me my driver and I tee up. I pull the tee up out of the ground like a reverse syringe, a full half-ball higher than I normally do. As I ready my swing, I grip the club with tight, closed wrists. In my backswing, I make sure I'm going straight up, then straight down with the club, following through to my left.

In short, I do my utmost to screw up this shot, blasting it so far off course that it will never be found.

The shot is perfectly terrible. Off it goes, far and to the right like a broken missile, and I muster up a false groan of disappointment.

"Youch," Lane says.

"That's my only ball. We gotta look for it," I tell him, fully confident that we won't find the ball and we will need to stay at Serenity forever, here on the Dancing Bull course, just him and me and Monty.

But then, about two hundred yards down, I see a ball lob onto the fairway from a small stand of trees.

"It kicked out!" Lane shouts. "You see that?! Member's bounce!"

Of course it did.

"Did you see?" Lane asks me again.

"No questions allowed," I grumble, and we drive on.

There is no earthly way this golf ball found its way through all the tree boughs and branches and trunks and roots to land on the fairway. It's a joke the Golf Gods are playing on me, because as soon as I want to leave this never-ending sequence of golf courses, they make sure I stay, and as soon as I want to stay, they make me play on. I pick up the ball and examine it: it's not mine. Someone has blacked out the brand name on the ball with a straight line, then turned it into a set of barbells. A reminder from beyond to be strong, perhaps? Why else would it be barbells?

We each bogey the second hole, carrying the skin over to the third, which means the winner gets two questions.

Still determined to prolong the round, I slice the shit out of my ball again on the third, skipping it three times across the water, but it refuses to break the surface of the pond and instead bounds to the other side.

Lane runs into some trouble, launching a wedge shot well over the green, but he saves it and gets double-bogey. I can get two questions with a decent, straight-ahead eight-foot putt, but instead I push the putt left and it rings around the lip before getting spit out. I tap in for double-bogey and the fourth hole is worth three questions.

I finally lose my ball on the fourth.

There's a construction site visible from the tee box, but it's way, way to the right, past the fairway toward the ninth. I don't even bother slicing the ball to try and disguise my intent. I aim far, far to the right and nail it with a big top-down drive. Lane and I watch my tee shot sail majestically into the clearing, like a soda can tossed into ocean waves. The ball disappears into the cluster of construction equipment and mounds of excavated earth.

"That," Lane says, "was an incredibly bad shot."

"Thank you," I tell him. "Can't golf if I don't have a ball."

"There's one right there," Lane says, and points at a spot almost exactly where my ball would have left the boundaries of the course. We drive to it and I hop out, fully expecting it to be my ball, but it's not. Instead, it bears a gigantic red "3" emblazoned on it with a marker.

"No penalty," Lane says. "Play it from here."

Fine. If the Golf Gods are going to make me play, I may as well win so I can find out more from Lane. I eye up the shot carefully this time, choose the 5-iron, and scorch the shot, getting on the green from about a hundred and eighty-five yards away.

Lane shoots me a look of surprise. "Where did that come from?" he says. "Sorry. Tough not to ask questions."

We get to Lane's yellow ball in the middle of the fairway and about a hundred and twenty yards out. He takes a 7-iron—which I can use to hit at least one-fifty—and hits it fat, which is to Lane's benefit as the ball rolls up to the fringe of the green.

"Looks like we got ourselves a putt-off," Lane says in a cowboy drawl.

We each putt twice and par the hole. Carry. Four skins on the next hole.

The fifth is a par-3. Lane grabs my fairway wood and tees off. I can't believe my eyes. He's put a whole bunch of topspin on it, creating a low trajectory. It lands fifty yards short of the green, then rolls straight ahead like a remote-controlled car, between the two bunkers and up a mound, then dies to the left as it rolls, then slows, then curls, right into the cup. Ace.

"Whaaaaaat?!" Lane exalts. "Bye-Bye, Mon Cowboy! Can you believe that?"

"Somehow I can," I say to him. "That's question one. You've got three left."

"You need to shoot. You could still get a hole in one."

"Sure I can." It's a formality. I toss my ball onto the ground and decide to lose it again. The farmer's fence still abuts the course on our right, so I nail the ball and it goes over a second time.

"Question two, hit me," I tell Lane before the ball has even landed in the wheat field.

"What do you tell Payne about me?"

Payne asks me if Mom is ever going to get back to normal.

"I'm sure it's just a matter of time," I tell him, but I don't believe it even as it comes out of my mouth. "You're never the same. But the black hole inside you gets point-one percent smaller, every day. Losing your dad is a big one, kid. At least for her, it is."

"How long did it take you to get back to normal after Lane died?" he says as he scoops another spoonful of cereal into his mouth.

"I don't know. Not as long as Mom is taking." I refrain from telling him I think it's been long enough, that grief needs to end and living needs to begin again. That I miss her too.

Payne never met my brother. Faith only knew him for a couple of years herself. We never talk about him anymore. His memory fades away, lost to the tides.

What would Lane have become to us, if he had come home alive?

Another ball appears as we walk toward the farm fence.

This one has another marking that looks like a barbell. There are no surprises.

"He knows about you," I lie. "He knows how important you were to me. Your energy …" my voice trails off. "I could talk about you till I'm blue in the face, Lane, but it will never be the same as knowing you. Also, it doesn't mean he'll listen. He's seventeen and addicted to the internet. You wouldn't believe what phones are like now."

"You tell him how opposite we were?"

"That's usually how it comes up. He doesn't seem to give a shit about anything, same as you."

"You think that's just like me?"

"I do. And that's question four. Onward," I say and Lane realizes he blew it with half of his questions. "Congrats on the hole in one."

Lane's golf luck doesn't last long: his ball finds sand on the sixth hole and he can't rescue it within the confines of par, which is four. I play the next hole a bit better, but not enough to beat a bogey. We tie and the skin carries over.

I lose my ball again on the seventh, this time without malice of forethought. I simply strike it with too open a club face and the ball hooks right into a dense bush. Lane and I both search inside the thicket but come up empty, then walk a perimeter around the bush in case my ball took a carom into some unseen place. Perhaps this time there will be no divine golf ball providence.

But lo, I spy another ball, sitting in the thatch and partially obscured, but I notice the marking is an angled greater-than sign, >, not a three or a "therefore." I guess I'm following the trail of a mathematician who loses a lot of golf balls. I decide to keep searching, pretending not to see it, afraid that I won't be able to make this last as long as I want it to.

"Look at this," Lane says, approaching from behind me and scooping up the ball I just deliberately chose to ignore. "Define prominence."

"What?"

"I mean like somebody's looking out for you."

"Oh my god, do you mean 'divine providence'?"

"No, I mean 'define prominence,' like can you believe how prominent your luck is right now, because here's another fucking golf ball for you to hit, exactly when you need it, like it was put there for you."

So I play another mathematically-marked ball to the end of the seventh, and the skin carries over once again, making the eighth worth three questions. If I win, I'll need to narrow down my list. I'm not sure I'll ever run out of questions for the ghost of my brother.

I am not playing well, even when I try. I don't know if the competition with Lane has me flustered, or if it's the constant attempts to spin my shots out of bounds. Or maybe it's that I don't care about golf as much as I did the round before, or the round before that.

I'm not in pain anymore, thankfully, but that means I can't use it as an excuse. It's me.

Determined to win the three skins, I summon up all the focus I can muster and take a deep breath, staring into the shaft of my driver as though I might imbue it with some magical good-golfing energy. I try to think about all the elements of my long-draw swing: ball lined up with inside of left heel, aim a bit right, sit down a little, straighten my back, waggle, open grip with flexing wrist, loosen grip, pull back, left shoulder down, right shoulder up like a water pump, then a swing from the inside of the ball and out, but not farther out than the angle of the open club face. Those are the ingredients and I put them all together, but the bread doesn't bake. My shot starts right and doesn't come back left, goes up as high as a bird, then lands hard like a penguin in flight and barely rolls at all. Total distance is probably less than two hundred yards.

Lane effortlessly drives his ball and opens up a fifty-yard advantage on me. That's the difference between a difficult 4-iron and an easy seven. But I'm determined to win, so I plug in the same formula to hit the long iron. Again, I loft it and I realize it's because my hands are too far in front of the ball. But the damage is done. I'm at least a hundred yards away from the green. Lane skies his shot with the much more workable 7-iron; it's a long and floating shot that seems to drift to the green and hover down like a flying saucer, easy and perfect, like he always was.

Lane hops back into the cart and I start it up. "Not sure I have three more questions," Lane gloats.

"Come on, Lane. I have so many questions for you. Please."

"Hey, I can't help it if you suck at golf. Rules are rules." I have had enough of the mockery. Suddenly it's like Lane never left.

"You always do this, Lane. You always rub it in my face."

"What do I rub? Who's rubbing?"

"You're rubbing! That's all you do. You show me how easy it is for you. Everything you do, it's 'Hey, this is easy,' but it *never* is for me. Never."

"Big brother syndrome strikes again," Lane says. He spits

onto the grass from the moving power cart, as some kind of punctuation. "Things are so tough for the big brother. Well, look at you. Wife. Kid. Home. Cottage. Money. Golfing all the time. A fucking life. Yeah, let me pity you some more, James. Tell me more about how 'life' is so hard for you."

The way he says "life" is like a knife in my belly.

Lane looks like he's on the verge of tears. I'm telling my tale of woe to my dead brother. I guess hard years look a lot better than no years.

"I'm sorry."

"You should be sorry," Lane says. "I make it look easy because I want to help you, James. I know how hard it is for you sometimes. I know how scared you get. I always knew."

"I'm not scared …"

"Horseshit. It's okay that you're scared. I wanted to make it better for you, man. Show you it's not as hard as you think. But you were always jealous. You took it wrong every time. You lived, James. Easy or tough, it was better than me."

We stop at my ball. I don't get out of the cart.

"Have you been here for all this time since …?"

"Now that," Lane says, "is a question. And I can't answer questions until you take some skins off me." Lane taunts me despite his tears. I want to touch his face.

Now that it barely matters, I strike a near-perfect wedge shot onto the green and it finishes sweetly, maybe six feet from the hole. But Lane has a putter in his hand already for his third shot. He doesn't sink his first putt, which gives me a chance to carry it over to the ninth. I let him tap in, leaving me a four-foot putt, which, after much deliberation, I proceed to hammer off to the left of the cup, not even close. Lane wins again.

This time, Lane ponders silently for a moment, playing up the pondering with a stroke of an invisible beard.

"Next hole, let's go," I mutter.

"Oh, don't be like that," Lane tells me. "Be a sport. Now hmm … *hmmmmm* …" he strokes his nonexistent beard cartoonishly as we sit down in the cart. "I got the first question: what is the number one thing you miss about me? No joking, I'm being serious."

"Number one …" I consider his question. "I guess I grew up thinking I was always going to have a little brother, you know? It never occurred to me that you wouldn't be close. So I guess the number one thing I miss is just having you around."

"Loving the honesty, but what about it is such a big deal? That's what I don't get."

"You don't get why having a person, who was your follower and helper and protégé and victim—you don't get why I might feel their absence when they disappear to the other side of the world and then die? You don't get that?"

"Question," Lane reminds me with a wagging finger and a singsong voice. "Speaking of which, I guess I got one left, huh?" He catches himself. "That was rhetorical."

"I'll allow it."

"Final question: James Khoury, if that's your real name, do you know why you are here?"

"You have the honour," I urge Lane out of the cart and onto the ninth tee.

"Answer the question." He grabs the driver and heads for the tee box.

"Because ... because Faith cut the logos out of my Hall of Fame that I spent my whole life putting together? Because she's mad ... but I don't know why." I don't want to admit that I know why she did it. Best to think about other things. "I still don't have an answer for any of it, do I?"

"Well, that's because you haven't won a question yet," Lane says. He tees off without preparation and skies his shot up in the air with so much backspin, it goes backward a couple of feet after it lands. Finally, on the ninth hole, I have an opening. I don't have to play well, just average, and I do. I look at Lane and his face registers some consternation. He's trying hard to prevent me from winning. That's a relief.

The hole is a longer par-4, a few challenges to be wary of but a fairly orthodox, flat layout ending in a moderately sloped green. The grooming here is excellent, perhaps aided by the mountain air and excessive irrigation of the Alberta foothills. I visualize my most reasonable course of action—5-iron, gap wedge, one six-foot putt—and it comes to pass: the 5-iron is straight and rolls to the right of a fairway bunker, leaving forty yards for a wedge shot that I place seven feet from the pin, but it spins back and rolls down the slope, leaving me with a six-foot putt. Lane's ninth hole is erratic and it takes him five shots to get where I am. There's no pressure at all. I lag the putt so I'm inches away, then tap in.

Lane doesn't even finish the hole. He picks up and approaches me.

"Well that's it, then," Lane taps my shoulder. "Let's have your question."

I don't even think about what I'll ask. It erupts from the depths of me. "Why did you leave?"

"There's no answer to that question, for anybody. Ask another one."

"I mean why did you go to Australia?"

"I left because it was time for me to go." Lane hands me my putter and his golf ball. "It's been amazing, man. So great. Now it's time for you to go and get right with your people."

Lane extends his hand for a handshake. A round-ending handshake.

"But we only played nine," I plead with him. "And Monty's Rut is the best part of this course. Please, just a bit longer."

"This is all we get."

"How do I make it right? I have more questions, Lane. We need more time."

Lane takes a final look into my eyes.

"Lane. Please! Please."

Lane grabs my hand and forcibly shakes it. Then he pulls me in for a tight embrace and I fall apart on his shoulder. "Don't leave me," I blubber into him. "Don't leave again."

"Good game, buddy," Lane says. "Catch you on the flip."

TOTAL SKINS: 8   SCORE: LANE 7, JAMES 1

"It's like you're not even here," I whisper as the credits roll on the screen.

"I'm sad," Faith says to me in the weakest voice.

"You gotta find some joy, hon. You're still alive."

"I know."

I swallow my words, but as the next episode in the stream fires up, they come out anyway.

"When?"

Faith says nothing.

"When are you going to be okay, Faith?"

Faith rises from her chair.

"You should be okay by now. The grief ... it's not happening the way it should, I think ..."

She stops and looks at me with those searing ice-blue eyes. She can't say anything. Maybe it's because she knows I'm right. Or maybe it's because I make things worse. She bolts for the bedroom.

"We're still alive, Faith. We get to live."

I let the words hang in the hallway, echoing. I hear her turn the shower on. She takes a lot of showers these days.

I switch to the Golf Channel.

Payne walks into the room, transfixed by his phone. He sees me crying, watching golf like it's some kind of numbing agent.

His reflex is to return directly to his subterranean lair.

9

CROWBUSH, 2003
Prince Edward Island: Eighteen Holes
Thomas McBroom

I use my forearm to wipe the curtain of steamy tears from
my eyes. The view comes into focus: sandy dunes pressed
up against the ocean tide, with lush greenery laid through
the sand like a necklace of tumours.

I am on Prince Edward Island, half an hour from
Charlottetown, and I remember The Links at Crowbush
Cove well because it's one of McBroom's most beloved
designs. One of McBroom's greatest talents is using the
natural terrain to create challenges for the golfer that don't
simulate nature, but embrace it. He finds ways to remind
the golfer that this is all by design, and that the designer
has considered your foray through this course with the
diligence of a diamond appraiser.

This place is an expression of the human relationship

with the physical world, in all its intemperate beauty. I first saw The Links at Crowbush Cove on TV when it hosted a skins game in the late nineties. It's a thrill to be here in the flesh with clubs in hand, ready to see what I can do with the sequence of tests McBroom has laid here.

I clearly remember playing Crowbush. I remember the logo on my shirt. But this doesn't feel like a memory. I am actually here. And Lane isn't. It rained when I played Crowbush, off and on—a gentle, chilling rain. The clouds look the same as they did that day: low and pregnant, ready to release in short bursts.

The weather isn't the only reason being at Crowbush chills me. I'll never forget what happened here.

The grass here is greener; the bentgrass is so lush it looks edible. At the first tees, you're instantly reminded of how this course will interact with water; the ocean is all around you at Crowbush, and a pond sits at the start of the first fairway like a soupçon of what's to come. "Sally Forth" is the name of this hole, and it's all you can do, isn't it?

And so I do. All us humans, we all want to do what we're meant to do. Maybe I'm meant to golf.

I crouch down to the side of my golf bag and reach into the pocket for a ball. I still only have the one. When I stand back up, I'm not alone.

"James Khoury, from Winnipeg, right?" It's Fiona, my caddie from across the Gulf of St. Lawrence at Cabot Cliffs.

"This isn't right," I utter, like somebody might be listening. The two courses aren't so far apart that Fiona couldn't be here. But she's still wearing her caddie coveralls, white from head to toe, and this time she's brought a set of clubs for herself.

But I golfed here in 2003.

Fiona glances past my right shoulder. "Looks like we're three," she says, and I turn to see a figure behind me, with perfect salt-and-pepper hair, rising up from behind his bag, making adjustments to his equipment.

Chi-Chi.

"Hey, bud," Chi-Chi says to me, like he expected me to be his golf buddy in Prince Edward Island, three thousand kilometres from home. He slides a couple of tees into the tee holders he's got on his pull cart.

My arms want to reach for him and bring him in. Take him back with me to Faith and Payne. Show him how much we all miss him. Another part of me wants to scream and throw fists at him for leaving us how he did. He was addicted to his work, leading his team of boys from construction job to construction job, making millions for a family who never shared enough of it with him. Chi-Chi never got what he deserved, and now his whole family knows there's no such thing as justice.

In the end, he fell like a leaf, turning over and over in the air as he made his way down to the concrete floor, so far below. A leaf is dead as soon as it is released from its life-giving tree. We like to think of Chi-Chi that way: as soon as he was let go, he was gone. There shouldn't have been any pain from the impact. Not the way we all felt it, and even if we're being delusional about how much he suffered, that statement is still true. Our pain remains, shaping us. Twisting us at the root.

He leaves. We remain.

Chi-Chi and me, we didn't get out to the course enough, but we talked golf every time we sat down together. At family gatherings, we'd talk about Tiger or Rory or Freddie Couples, and that weekend's tournament coverage would be featured on the television screen like wallpaper.

I had planned to take a long weekend or two that summer and make my way to Kenora for a few rounds as a new member's guest at Beauty Bay. It never happened. Instead, we all gathered at the Kenora Golf and Country Club, in the banquet hall, putting on brave faces and telling quippy anecdotes to soothe our grief. When Faith stood at the podium and held back her tempest of emotions to speak, a bolt of lightning cracked through the sky like a chisel into marble, and thunder proclaimed to all of us that something up there was taking part in this ceremony. They had to clear all the golfers off the course, to the delight of the funeral-goers, who saw it as a fitting tribute. And Faith knew it was Chi-Chi, helping her along with her speech. We all raised our glasses to the sky. But now he is here, which means that thunder is just thunder, and the words Faith said were never heard by the sky, and Chi-Chi could not have possibly pulled the strings from behind those clouds. Something in my stomach sinks a bit lower.

"What are you doing here?" I manage to say through my stupefaction before my jaw decides to quit receiving any type of signal from my brain.

Chi-Chi's ear-to-ear grin erupts across his face and he holds up his ball.

"What does it look like?" he says to me, dipping his head in the slightest way to let me know it's time to play.

Maybe he could be in two places at once, behind the

clouds and right in front of me. Maybe it *was* him, operating the clouds like a wizard: all-powerful, all-knowing ... maybe he even knows about Chi-Chi's Longest Shot.

First my dead brother, and now my dead father-in-law, golfing, in the flesh, right in front of me. Exactly what am I supposed to do with this information? Should I tell him about all the lives he's left cracked, the emptiness he left behind, like slithering trenches in the soil where the roots of an oak once stood? Now absence is present. Absence is trying to hit a shapely drive and keep it on the fairway, and I am trying to simply keep my mind from spinning off into the gulf.

Chi-Chi is a lefty and a big hitter. But it's his first drive of the day and he puts too much shape on it, hooking the shot too far off to the right. His ball careens into the black spruces, not far from an old wooden shed.

"It's a start," Chi-Chi says. It'll take more than an imperfect golf shot to take his smile away. He pivots on his bow-leg like a pumpjack and picks his tee up out of the ground, all in a single, smooth motion like he's done for probably fifty years.

The entire time I prepare to take my tee shot, I try to figure out exactly what to say to Chi-Chi. Are Fiona and I supposed to help him leave this mortal plane or something? Is Fiona supposed to help me help Chi-Chi, like she's maybe a guardian angel trainer? Is that why I just golfed with Lane?

I'm focused on what to say as I place a perfect drive on the fairway; it's a thing of nearly tear-rending beauty when your intention is reflected precisely through the sky and onto the smooth lawn of the fairway.

This isn't that. My shot possessed no intention at all. It just goes like a bastard.

"Ho-ly crow!" Chi-Chi says lyrically as he admires my shot. "You been practicing, huh?" I missed that smile.

Almost instantly, Fiona is at the red tees. Chi-Chi stands beside me. The silence as she tees off is like a vacuum, begging to be filled with all my questions and laments, but I manage to let the moment pass. "Well," Chi-Chi murmurs, like a piece of punctuation, and we get walking.

My shot is closer to Fiona's, and as Chi-Chi pulls away to the right, Fiona falls into step beside me.

"I'm here to help you," she says to me.

"Help me with what, Fiona? Are you my training angel or something? Is this golf heaven?"

She doesn't say a word, just gives me a flummoxed look with the wrinkles around her eyes, like she doesn't know what I'm talking about. The question surprises her.

"When you listen to golfers, you'll come to the conclusion that golfing is merely what we do with nature," she says to me with that maritime lilt. "Golf, b'y." She tees up in exactly the same way Krista teed up during the round we played here.

"I know why I'm here," I say. Though I'm looking at Fiona, in my mind, I see Krista twisting through her languid warm-up swing.

"Relax," Fiona says. "You're okay. It's all okay." With barely any preparation and an address that looks more like a how a person addresses a roadside mailbox than a golf ball—back bent and butt sticking straight out—Fiona smoothly delivers a low 3-wood that rolls perfectly up the middle of the fairway.

"Everything will be hunky-dory," she says.

Chi-Chi plays it where it lies, craftily working the same-shaped shot so that it lands on the green.

"It's fine," Krista says. "You're okay. It's all okay."

She gets closer, so that the shaft of her iron is resting on my thigh.

I step back and try to address the ball, instead of addressing the hot breaths of temptation sticking to my chest hair.

The memory slaps me in the face, and I take an unsteady step back from the green. Luckily I'm able to make it look like I'm just sizing up my putt. Chi-Chi is waiting for me to go before he walks across the green to his ball, so as not to cross my line of vision. That space is sacrosanct in this game. You don't violate that space.

It occurs to me that I no longer remember my last shot.

The wind stiffens, carrying a chill on its back as it whips through the pines. We tidy up our putts and head to the next hole, travelling deeper into the forest.

The second hole is a standard par-4, tree-lined and moderate. But when you reach the green, the slope at the back half of the dance floor is nasty. Today, the flag shoots straight back, pin barely visible on the downside of the green. It's an impossibility, this pin placement.

Krista extends her arms out, like she's embracing the wind. Her shirt billows to the left. She turns her head back to smile at me, to cast her joy where it can reel me in. Clearly, the wind is entertaining her. I'm focused on the hidden hazards coming into view.

"So how's everybody?" Chi-Chi says to me as we trudge to our parallel tee shots.

"Everybody? Who's everybody?"

"The family—Faith, Payne ... Dorothy."

"Everybody's okay."

I dig through my own muddled memory to try and find a more honest answer.

Faith? She's not the same, Chi-Chi. I don't know where she went.

I feel like Payne wants to see me about something, like we didn't get a chance to connect on something, like when you miss an appointment.

Dorothy's trying to follow the Longest Shot, all the way to Scotland.

I don't tell him any of this. What keeps a person busy, after your other half of a half-century goes, is a process they call "the handling of affairs." Dorothy had to pick up after Chi-Chi and address all the thousands of things he left behind. There had been a dump truck full of things for Dorothy to donate to the second-hand store or homeless shelter or landfill. A literal dump truck full. Every item was like a scissor-snip to her, cutting at her insides a tiny bit, each one, ten thousand scissor-snips as she threw away all the things that belonged to Chi-Chi. Ten thousand reminders that there's no justice and no goodbye. Only gravity.

The golf equipment was the worst. Chi-Chi kept all of his stuff in a shed in the backyard and it was his most sacred domain. It was the last place Dorothy went to sort things out. She knew there would be friends and sons-in-law who would happily take good care of these things. But Dorothy also remembered what Chi-Chi said about his golf balls, about how he visualized them to go where he wanted them to go, and so there was a tiny bit of his soul inside of every golf ball he hit.

It was the hokiest thing she had ever heard. You can't put your soul in a golf ball by hitting it! Stupid man.

But if Chi-Chi believed it, then maybe Dorothy would do something as a modest tribute. She would take one of his golf balls and send it farther than Chi-Chi could ever imagine: the Longest Shot.

Chi-Chi's best friend Dave was heading east to Etobicoke for a business trip and was planning to golf at St. George's, one of Canada's top courses. Dorothy gave him one of Chi-Chi's most used, dinged-up balls, and asked him to lose that ball on the golf course.

Dave didn't lose the ball at St. George's. Instead, he was paired up with a man from St. John's who offered to take Chi-Chi's ball and lose it in the Atlantic, knowing Dorothy's intent for the ball to go as far as it could. Dave agreed, and when he told Dorothy, she thought it was an impressive distance for a tiny piece of Chi-Chi's soul to travel, because it's amazing what happens to your perspective when your most-beloved leaves, suddenly and unexpectedly, and all you have left is what they leave behind, including their idiotic philosophies on what you can do with a gull dang golf ball.

A few weeks later, Dave visited Dorothy to deliver a a printed-out email from his friend in St. John's. The friend wrote that he had been in a pub on George Street and toasted Chi-Chi, with every intention of launching the ball into the Atlantic from Cape Spear, but got well into his cups and told some drinking buddies Chi-Chi's story, and how Dorothy wanted his final shot to travel as far as it could. The whole pub raised a glass to him and the poor family he left behind. A fitting tribute, Dorothy thought, and imagining that toast made her warm inside. Dave prodded her to read on. The man in St. John's had closed the bar down with an elderly couple from Scotland. St. Andrews, Scotland, to be precise. Now there's no ranking of saints, as far as I know, but in golf, Saint Andrew is the patron saint of saints. Dave's impromptu golf partner gave Chi-Chi's ball to the Scots, and the Scots had promised to write when they made it back home to St. Andrews and lost Chi-Chi's ball on the course somewhere.

But Chi-Chi's ball was never lost. No ball ever is, I suppose; it's only off-course—lost to you. A letter came a month later, care of Dave once again, bearing a post-mark from Scotland. Dave was happy to see a smile return to Dorothy's face as she ripped the envelope from the Scottish couple open. But her brow furrowed as she read: the ball wasn't in St. Andrews. The husband had taken ill and they were waylaid in Edinburgh. The wife wrote a profuse apology, explaining that she couldn't travel to St. Andrews given the state of things. However, they had made the decision to visit The Sheep Heid Inn, the oldest pub in Scotland, and have a final drink together before the husband started his chemotherapy, making a toast to Chi-Chi in the meantime. The bartender overheard and offered to take the ball and leave it marinating in a jar of three-hundred-year-old whisky that no one was ever going to drink, on display atop the bar.

The Longest Shot. Distance: 6.2 million yards.

"That ball has gone a long way," Dave told Dorothy. "Only fitting it would end in a bar. Maybe someday we can go get a drink with Chi-Chi at his bar in Scotland."

But Dorothy had a strange, new desire. Suddenly, she wanted the ball back.

Her fixation made Dorothy impossible to cope with, and it wasn't long before Faith's damage came head-on with Dorothy's damage. They overwhelmed each other until they stopped speaking entirely, Chi-Chi would have rained down thunderbolts if he knew.

Instead of telling Chi-Chi any of this, I lie to him and say everyone is great, and hit an over-lofted approach shot that hangs in the air forever, buoyed by the stiff winds. My shot comes down well past the hole, panging off the cart path and into the bush.

"You taking care of yourself?" Chi-Chi asks, which is how he always asks about you.

"Not bad for an old man," is always my reply, a line I stole from my grandpa.

I grab another ball from my pocket—one with a marking that looks like a heavy barbell—and replay the shot.

"Old man? Old is merely a state of mind, bud."

"Then I guess you can call me Methuselah," I tell him.

His smile makes my neck warm. I firm up my downward focus and address my re-shot, trying to contain a grin of my own. It lands on the green before I realize: I only had one ball to play. I have no idea how this ball ended up in my pocket.

I remember what I want to remember, Faith tells me all the time.

Chi-Chi is on his way to a birdie on the par-5 third hole. I'm flirting with disaster on either side of the fairway, doing a military march along its edges: left, right, left.

Fiona seems to hang back, letting me have this time with Chi-Chi.

"Love golf," I say to fill a silent moment. I suppose it's a replacement statement, like "lovely weather," rather than telling Chi-Chi, "Hey, do you realize I must have lost my damn mind because there's no way you could possibly be here?"

"What's not to love?" Chi-Chi says to me. I wonder if that's a replacement statement for him too. "This game, man. It gets into your bloodstream." He taps his temple. "Rewires you, up here."

When we get to the green, I notice Chi-Chi still has that dime he uses to mark his putts.

I pull my ball marker out of my pocket: same dime, I think.

Chi-Chi thrashes both Fiona and me by the time we head back toward the clubhouse and the ninth hole. He masters the slopes. He carries every pond and pot bunker. He's enjoying the terrain. I've barely noticed the ocean and beaches. The wind chills me.

Fiona plays her game quietly, trying to keep her distance. She doesn't have to tell me I'm losing my focus. I know it.

"Faith still golfing?" Chi-Chi asks, and I shake my head. "Not really."

Chi-Chi bristles as he surveys the sweep and roll of the fairway that drops away into a blind valley, right around the two-hundred-yard mark. "You know, a couple needs to share things. It's a lot more fun when you're not inside of yourself for four hours."

"I need to be focused," I tell him. "It's okay. I like to be alone, sometimes. So does Faith."

"Golfing alone isn't healthy."

"Neither is working when you're seventy."

He tees off. Things get quiet.

We climb up the long staircase to the eleventh tees, me and Chi-Chi. We aren't speaking.

This tee box surveys the entire course and its ocean backdrop, giving us a jaw-dropping panorama. It's the most magnificent vista at Crowbush. I remember it well.

"Wow," Krista says to me. "This makes me weak in my knees."

I shake my head.

"Yeah, it's nice."

"Come on, boss. Take your shot."

Fiona, Chi-Chi, and I golf together, but separately. Together but separate is my specialty. I'm playing horribly and the soreness in my back returns, no doubt from pulling my cart through the swales and mounds of this links-style track.

The pain and exertion, combined with the saltwater gusts, parches me and chaps my lips. Fiona stands at a water station, filling cone-shaped paper cups.

"Water?" she says, but there's a firmness in her voice like she's not offering, but insisting. I take the water and pound it back. It's not nearly enough so I take the other one too. She heads back to the water cooler. And that's when my heart nearly leaps into my throat.

"I get it," I tell her. "I'm seeing ghosts. This is like a séance."

She brings two more cups, raising one to my mouth like she's going to feed me the water herself.

"You take it easy, Mr. Khoury."

On the eighteenth, I look at Chi-Chi, who hasn't spoken to me for two hours. With a single sideways glance from Fiona, it occurs to me that I've wasted the time I've got left with him. This sequence will end, and I'm sure I'll be on to the next hallucination or brush with death or whatever this is. And Chi-Chi will be gone. Is he supposed to have some kind of message for me? Or me, him?

How am I supposed to get back to the real world from here?

Maybe Chi-Chi's message is: "Don't mess around behind my daughter's back." He doesn't need a lot of words to convey that particular statement.

I change my focus.

"Payne is so different now. You'd barely recognize him."

Chi-Chi doesn't say anything. He looks down the shaft of his driver, like it's a rifle scope, aiming it at the pin some four hundred and sixty-four yards away.

"I barely recognize him myself these days, so after two years, he'd be a complete stranger to you."

Chi-Chi rounds behind his ball, then steps carefully alongside it for his address.

"You tell him to be a good boy," Chi-Chi says. "Tell him Gramps says to listen to his folks, eat his cereal, get to bed before midnight."

I don't know what to do with this information; Chi-Chi

seems to have known all along that he's dead. I look to Fiona for guidance but all she does is fumble around with her golf bag, completely unmoved by what he said.

"Nothing intelligent happens after midnight," Chi-Chi says. He launches the drive and it's a beauty, rising steadily, visibly accelerating like some kind of winged machine. Its mild right spin takes him back from the middle-left to the middle-right of the fairway, a couple of yards shy of three bean-shaped bunkers that look like a father, daughter, and child. Three generations of bunker. It's a perfect left-handed drive from beginning to end.

After midnight.

The words unlock something in my memory, something dark and shaking, like a found-footage film or an accidental smartphone video:

I run down the hallway in the middle of the night. Into Payne's room. I fling open the door and Payne isn't there. His computer is on, playing loud music. The curtains billow in the night air. The bug screen is missing from the window.

"Oh. You gotta like that one, bud," Chi-Chi says. "Gotta love it."

I stand there and stare, unable to throw an expression at him. As he walks past, he rests a hand on my shoulder. "Play along," Chi-Chi whispers in my ear.

I look at him and Chi-Chi looks back but doesn't say a word. He simply quirks his eyebrows and nods his head surreptitiously. *Play along?* Then he gives a furtive glance toward Fiona and mouths something silently. I can't be sure, but I think he's mouthing "help her." *Help Fiona?* Chi-Chi slides his driver back in the bag.

"Mr. Khoury, you're up. Let's go, please," Fiona calls out.

I scramble to get up to the tee box and fire off a drive, barely paying any attention to what I'm doing. Of course, once I stop thinking about it, the ball leaps off of my club face and I'm only twenty yards back of Chi-Chi's shot.

Fiona lurches past us, dragging her cart like she's dragging a misbehaving kid out of a store. She grumbles to herself, "You're not the only one that needs tending to." What's that supposed to mean?

I must be completely insane. I am now of the belief that I am some type of ghost communicator, and Fiona is my supervisor or assistant … or caddie?

As Fiona heads for the front-most tees, Chi-Chi nudges me. "You gotta cooperate, bud. They're trying to help."

"Who the hell is 'they,' Chi-Chi? Am I supposed to help you cross over or something? Why aren't you in heaven?"

Chi-Chi steps back like maybe I said something insulting. "What if this *is* heaven, bud? If it is, why would *you* be here?" A frigid maritime gust pushes against us like it heard him. I get a chill.

Fiona looks back and Chi-Chi shuts up, as though we're two inmates and she's our guard. We start moving. She tees off and it's a goner, a hook shot right into the pond. "Go again," Chi-Chi shouts at her.

"You need to get yourself out of this," Chi-Chi says under his breath, and the pain in my back flares suddenly, like fire twisting down my spine and into my thighs. I gasp and curl into myself.

Ahead of us, Fiona smashes her driver into the grass and it bounces up and out of her hands. She puts her hands on her hips and steps away. She looks at us and something in her face changes, like she's suddenly noticed something about me and Chi-Chi. She starts walking toward us.

"Shit," Chi-Chi says.

"What is she doing?" I ask him, but Chi-Chi is frozen in fear.

He turns to me suddenly. "I'll be okay," he says. "Listen," and he takes me by the arms like a child and looks into my eyes, his breath hot on my face. "I'm sorry for how it happened but I'm okay. Now you gotta go back. Back to *them*. And the only way to do that is for you to play it out. To play along. To play through. Your round isn't done."

"I don't understand."

"I'm fine. Don't worry about me. Payne. Faith. They need you. Now get going."

Fiona rushes toward us, concern etched on her face.

"I'm sorry but it looks like visiting time is over," she says.

"No!" I blurt and Chi-Chi yells something at that exact same moment. Fiona waves her arms at us like she's hailing a car on the highway, and suddenly night falls on Prince Edward Island, and my time with Chi-Chi is over.

I think Chi-Chi had yelled, "Read the ball." What's that supposed to mean?

Now that our round is over, I'm prepared for another instantaneous change of scenery. Every other time, it's like I've blinked and suddenly I'm golfing somewhere else.

This time, it's different. This time, things go black. And then then I see a face—brow creased with worry, eyes awash in tears—projected forty feet tall like she's on a drive-in movie screen.

Faith's face. She silently kicks her crossed leg, arms

folded, eyes sunken like pot bunkers fringed with the tall grass of sleeplessness. It's dawn. I'm yelling at Payne.

"Where the hell were you until four-thirty in the morning?"

"Adam's. We were playing some games."

"Did you think it would be okay to sneak out of your window and take off without telling us where you were going?"

"This time you caught me."

"What if something happened to you? If there's even the tiniest whiff of alcohol or anything on you, so help me ..."

Payne shrugs and looks at me with dead eyes. Makes me even more irate.

"A lot of nerve, kid. A lot of nerve. Faith, do you have anything to say about this?"

I look behind me. Faith is gone. She's starting a shower.

Payne gazes at his shoes.

"You are grounded, Payne. Your mother and I will decide how long after some sleep."

"Yeah, right."

"What did you just say?"

"Nothing."

We engage in a stare down: me staring at Payne's face, Payne starting at the carpet.

"I have a seven o'clock tee time. Expect bars on your windows when I get back from golf."

Payne piffles his lips at this. I try to ignore it.

"Dad, can I ask you something?"

"No, Payne. You've wasted enough of my time. Get to bed."

He skulks off. "And if you think you're sleeping all day," I call to him, "think again."

"Have fun golfing."
All I can come up with is a parental, "Payne!"
"You guys are like zombies. Why do you care all of a sudden where the fuck I went?"
Dramatic teenager door slam.

10

ÖVIINBYRD, 2017
Ontario: Eighteen Holes
Thomas McBroom

An earthen smell and distant pinging is all I need to know that I play on. And on and on.

It takes a second to register that my face is pressed to the earth like I'm genuflecting to some torturous deity, my rear end in the air and my hands outstretched. I scream into the ground in frustration and then let the pose collapse, falling to my side. Sunshine stabs me in the eyes again.

There were times in my life when I thought I could never tire of golfing. Finally, completely, I am golfed out. Please, take me home.

My eyes adjust to the shivs of sun and I slowly come to recognize where I've been placed: Karl's home course, Öviinbyrd, the crown jewel of Muskoka golf.

It was here that I went from being an admirer of McBroom's work to an actual fan. It's as though he uses unseen forces to create a course that is natural and supernatural at the same time. Every inch of a McBroom course is an interaction with something larger than humanity. Every shot, as you survey it, is a reminder of how incredibly weak and small we are. That delectable satisfaction of making the shot work—of making your intentions felt in the place where human and nature intertwine—there's no better feeling.

I have clear memories of the otherworldly experience at Öviinbyrd from when I got a chance to play here with Karl.

Laid upon the Canadian Shield like a royal robe, the course doesn't follow a traditional eighteen-hole looping format. It ventures out; far, far, out. When you reach the ninth and tenth holes, you're the farthest from home that you've ever been.

"There's something going on with you and Krista," Karl says to me as he stares down the cup on the ninth. He reaches down on one leg and fishes his ball out.

I know what he's talking about but I feign surprise.

"Oh my god, wipe your eyes and get up. So embarrassing," Payne's voice says, and the blinding sun reveals my son standing above me.

Payne is dead. Every muscle in my body burns.

"There's no way in hell," I say to the sky, to Fiona, or whoever is running this nightmare. "Send him back. Please send him back!" I squawk at nothingness.

"Back to where, Dad?" He offers me a hand up, and I take it.

"It's just that … I don't know what's happening. Are you—what happened?" Payne's eyes bug out. He looks at me like I'm an idiot, which is an expression he has nearly perfected in seventeen years of being my son.

"Khoury, two. Please make your way to the tees," a woman's voice crackles through a speaker. Not Fiona's, but familiar.

We look at each other for a moment. They're waiting for us. Being late when I'm expected somewhere makes me nauseous with unease. It's a trait Payne and I must share because when I reach for my pull cart I see that he already has a head start toward the empty tee box.

"Of course we're golfing," Payne says as he pulls his driver out. "Not like we'd be doing what I want to do, right?"

Chi-Chi told me to keep playing. I know I should wrap my arm around my son and try to find a way out of here. Instead, we fall into our pattern: we bicker.

"What would you want to do, Payne? Watch videos of people watching videos?"

Payne shakes his head and "whatever"s me. I've already ruined it. I can see his face sour and the bottom falls out of my stomach. I usually stick to my guns, because I'm the parent and he's the kid and what I say is therefore always right. This is not one of those times.

"I'm sorry," I tell him. "I don't know why I'm always this way with you, Payne."

He looks down, fidgets with his fingernails.

"But I have to be this way, I think."

I'm certain there's something Payne wants to say. But he shakes it off and continues the trek to the tee box, pulling my old clubs—the ones I'd tossed in the garbage—behind him. He's going to golf with me.

Now that he's a teenager, he's too cool for golf, but he learned enough at a young age that it comes back to him naturally. Back when he was eight or nine, I would take him with me to the Canoe Club on in-service days. It was the perfect arrangement: I would golf and he would drive the power cart, then hop out when there was time and space and shank a few balls down the fairway with his junior-sized 9-iron.

At Victoria Beach, Payne and I would ride our bikes from the cottage to the athletic fields, golf clubs in hand. Every Tuesday and Thursday, the kids would fight off the fishflies enough to turn the fields into a driving range. Some of those kids—the ones with the real privilege— could hit it right out of the field and into the lawns of the neighbouring cottages. Not Payne.

We got out to the VB Golf Course a couple of times before he decided to drop golf altogether.

Payne is taller than me now, with a fat bob of black hair and the hint of a moustache. People say he looks like me, but I don't see it. All I see is Faith, and maybe Chi-Chi, but lanky, without the years of toil on his back. It seemed to happen in bursts, every few months: I'd wake up and Payne would be replaced by a taller, clumsier version with Payne's voice, and then a few months later, the personality would shift and darken, and then the voice would change, and then the body again. And now here he is, a man in more ways than me, on some golf course beyond the grave, and I barely know him.

Under normal circumstances, it would be a dream

come true for me to be here with Payne on a golf course. I've missed it. It's probably been three years since he's held a club, and his form is anything but smooth and easy, but he gets the job done with his tee shot. He's not confident enough in his driver to use that, so he hits a 5-iron, and fires off a decently straight opener that lands on the fairway, but rolls to the right enough to get to the rough.

"Shit," he says, not caring, and picks up his tee.

That's when I see a black blob on the left side of his neck, from his shoulder to his earlobe.

"What. The fuck. Is that." My words hang in the air for a moment. Payne straightens back up, then looks at me like I'm an idiot.

"It's a pretty straightforward question, son."

"You mean the tattoo?"

I get closer to inspect and he doesn't withdraw. He raises his head and displays his neck to me like he's proud of it. The black blob is some kind of L-shaped, shafted implement.

"Is it a golf club?"

"Thanks a lot, *Dad*. Yeah, I'm gonna get a tat of a golf club."

He shuffles back to his pull cart, leaving me the tee box. I slide my tee into the grass, placing the ball marked with the greater-than symbol onto its launch pad, on the shoulder of the tee, all in a single, clinical motion.

"It's not a hockey stick ..."

"It's a sickle."

"Are you a Communist?"

"Don't be an asshole. You know, like the grim reaper?"

"A scythe," I inform him. "Did you draw it yourself?"

A grim reaper's scythe? Is Payne dead?

I put down my club and speak softly, as though our conversation might be monitored. "Payne, please listen to me."

He comes closer.

"This is no joke," I tell him. "I was just golfing with Grandpa."

"Oh my God." The disbelief oozes through him. "What are you even saying right now, Dad?" An almost-imperceptible twitch betrays him, in the corner of his eye. A troubled look when he thinks about Chi-Chi, maybe.

"Shh. Shh," I don't know who might listening in. "Before that, I was on another golf course, playing with Lane. Uncle Lane."

"Uncle Lane. Dad, you see the recurring thread through all of this, right? You're nuts."

"And now I'm here."

"And now you're here."

Payne purses his lips and looks down at his feet. "Dad," he says, softly. "This is a nice place, but me golfing with you is clearly nuts."

"I want to be wrong, Payne. I want to be, but I know I'm not. I've been presented with … incontrovertible evidence. This is some kind of afterlife-type deal."

"Okayyy," Payne says to me in the way only your teen child can; in the way that tells you he doesn't believe you and thinks you're an idiot and "whatever" to all of it. "So your response to finding out I got a tattoo on my neck is to tell me about your crazy-ass golf game visions?"

"I will give you supreme shit for the tattoo once I know what the hell is going on," I tell him.

"Oh my God, Dad. *Field of Dreams 2*, except your heaven is my hell. Golfing!" He laughs at the idea. "Shoot your ball, please. And then you can shoot me."

"Not funny." I pick up the driver and I hack at the ball carelessly. I'm ahead of Payne but off to the right as well. We'll walk together. Something in me intended that, which must have been passed on to the ball.

"Let's go, then," I tell him, and we walk. I try to find words, but none come.

As we get to his second shot, Payne murmurs, "It's fine, Dad. I'm fine."

"Okay," I say to him, and I don't push it.

Despite the beauty of our surroundings, there's no joy in this round for me. Payne says nothing and plays an erratic game, and I also couldn't care less about how well I'm golfing. All that bullshit about being the ball and focusing on the wrong thing: I flush it and smack the ball around.

The moist lake air is tinged with the aroma of charbroil. We leave the first few holes and head deeper into the forest, where spruce, jack pine, sugar maple, and tamarack each emit their own unique scents. The sunlight washes over all of it like a baptismal cleanse, including me and Payne. It's cool and clear today. Payne's plaid flannel reminds me of Lane: another grunge golfer, perhaps.

We see three deer—a buck, doe, and fawn—wandering through the bush on the fourth hole, at the edge of the course, where the human dominion over nature ends and the Ontario wilderness begins.

We don't speak for the better part of an hour. No murmurs to one's self, no congratulations or offers of advice.

Silence. Payne is like that fawn at the edge of the wilderness, and if I say anything too direct or honest, it'll spook him and he'll be gone forever.

He looks back at me grimly, like he's already planning some kind of retort for whatever I lob at him.

Payne's ball is about two feet from the cup after two putts. I'm away, about three feet from the hole still, but I let him finish up. He misses his third putt and curses to himself quietly.

"Gimme," I blurt awkwardly.

"What?"

"Close enough. It's a gimme from there, Payne. Pick it up."

He picks up his ball and eyes me. His glare is a split fingernail going up and down my spine as I try to finish my own putt. He's going to say something sarcastic and I brace for it, but nothing comes and I attempt the putt. The ball lips out. I pause for a moment, in case Payne returns the favour and gives me the gimme, but he doesn't and I tap in for a double-bogey.

"Don't you wonder why I got a grim reaper tattoo on my neck?"

"Are you in a gang now, or just making a lifelong commitment to unemployability?"

"Never mind." He turns away from me and walks from the green. I make my way to my bag and slide the putter in, then do my best to catch up.

"Payne," I call out to him. "I'm sorry. Tell me."

"You know when you get a song in your head, and the only way to get it out is to play the song and hear it out loud?"

"Yeah."

"Ever since Grandpa died, it was like a song that wouldn't go away ... everybody dies. Life isn't about living at all. It's about death. I couldn't stop thinking about it, doodling it, writing in my journals about it. I had to get it out of my head because ... I couldn't get the lights to come back on inside me."

I have forbidden Payne from labelling himself as "depressed." But this is certainly one way to describe depression. A poetic way.

Payne's eyes don't well up with tears. His brow doesn't furrow. He's so matter-of-fact about this that I can't say anything. I thought Payne was dealing with dumb teenager angst. But he's grappling with the same things Faith and I are dealing with.

While you were golfing. Asshole.

"It bugs me, Dad. There's more dead people than living people. We spend more time dead than alive. It's bigger than life. I needed to stop that song from singing, I guess."

"Why didn't you tell me when you thought there was a problem in the first place?"

"I tried to tell you, Dad. I tried a bunch of times."

"You did not."

"I did, like when I snuck out."

That shuts me up.

"Payne..."

Payne's voice drops ten decibels, "No surprise that I have to talk to you about it on a golf course."

I step forward, and Payne responds with a step back, clutching his own arms.

"I thought you were okay."

"No, you didn't. You didn't think anything about me. You were too busy escaping."

I look down at my shoes. *That has to change, right this minute.* But then I remember where we are—where we *really* are. We're not golfing.

Maybe pain isn't what makes us alive. Maybe pain is what shapes us for eternity.

Streams of tears have leaked from the dark corners of Payne's eyes. He looks like he hasn't slept in two years, and it's as troubling to me as if he had been cutting himself.

"Once this round of golf is done," I say quietly, "somebody's going to come and take you away."

I can feel those words twisting up my insides, making my tongue fatten inside my mouth. I can't swallow.

And then I remember Niakwa and my round with Scott Branch. We stopped for drinks. We stopped for massages. We stopped all the time.

"You know what? Let's see what happens if we sit for a second." I sit on the ground. Payne stands there, looking down at me for a couple of ticks. He looks to his left and right, scratches his temple, and then sits down too.

"We're not dead, though," he says.

"Payne, exactly what would a seventeen-year-old who knows nothing about the world but thinks he knows everything say in this situation right now? If you ask me, a seventeen-year-old would probably say he's not dead and his dad is completely wrong, even in the face of knowing nothing about anything."

"I didn't ask you."

He didn't. I nod in reluctant agreement, and so we sit

there. Birds chirp. The wind rattles the leaves on the trees like a warning that they will soon fall.

"Dad?" Payne says, after a time.

"Yes, son?" I try to keep my tone light.

"What happened to you?"

What happened to me? Life happened to me. I got old. Like a boa constrictor, time slowly slithers around you until it gets so tight that you go grey and feel ready to collapse. The boa gets everybody.

"You mean why wasn't I there for you when you needed me?"

Payne picks at the grass. "Sort of, I guess, but not only that. I mean, why weren't you there at all?"

I start to pick at the grass too. I don't have a good answer, so I try to give him my answer to everything.

"Getting old is horrible, Payne. But it's not the getting old that's so bad. It's almost like your mind and body let go of reality, bit by bit, so you can cope with how fast time goes, and how hard gravity and inertia and heat and cold can be on your body, and how everything you love—every single thing that draws a breath or grows in the light—all of it is going to die and leave you behind to mourn it. All the stuff"—I scoff here—"all the stuff you collect, like a house and a car and a set of steak knives ... a Hall of Fame ... it's all a distraction from the honest truth. Nobody's in control of anything. It's so deeply fucking terrifying."

Payne's face is wrenched into a displeased scowl. Maybe it's pensive, but it looks cranky.

"Getting old means knowing the truth and still finding a way to smile at people, and eat your breakfast, and find a moment that means something, while the disgusting truth of it all sits there on your back. And my back is weak, son. So sometimes I need to golf so I can stand up straight."

Payne rests his head in his hand and looks up at me with half-closed eyes. "Okay, Dad," he says, his tone so patronizing. When he says "Dad" like that it makes me nuts.

"What?"

"You didn't even try to answer my question, Dad, which is so incredibly you. I ask you a direct question and you immediately go back into your own shit."

"I didn't—"

"You so did. I'm sorry life has you sad, but ..." he chokes on something.

"Don't try to provoke me," I warn him.

And then the motorized whirr of a golf cart rumbles through the air. A red power cart, with the word "MARSHAL" written on the front in giant red letters, bounds into the clearing from a treed path, like some kind of forest predator. Instinctively, I get to my feet, because I know we're doing something a marshal would not condone. Sitting in the middle of the golf course isn't expressly forbidden in The Rules of Golf, but neither is running someone over with a power cart.

Inside the red marshal's cart are two figures. I recognize them as they approach: Fiona is in the passenger's seat. Beside her is a curly-haired woman in her mid-thirties with a sullen expression. She looks familiar, and realization hits me like a thunderclap: she worked at the pro shop. All of the pro shops.

Tricks of the memory.

The cart pulls up and they wait for the engine to quiet before Fiona speaks.

"You need to get playing, Mr. Khoury," she says to me in her East Coast lilt. Then she turns to Payne and motions for him to get up. "We can't have you sitting in the middle of the course. Please cooperate."

"What are you going to do, kick us out?" I ask her.

"Yes, please," Payne says, but he stands up anyway.

"I'm sure you'd like to keep spending time together, yes?" the other woman says with a noticeably French accent. Payne and I look at each other and realize that's true.

"Be respectful to others," the Frenchwoman says in a thundering voice. There's something threatening in it. "This place isn't just for you."

"This is LaBelle," Fiona says, "I need you two to listen to her, all right? She's in charge."

LaBelle's stare is so cold it almost knocks me backward. It makes Fiona's stern face seem friendlier.

"Is Payne dead, Fiona?"

"Oh my God, Dad," Payne murmurs and shields his face.

Fiona looks into my eyes, and her crow's feet tauten into a knowing smile. Whatever she knows, she's not telling.

"Please, Fiona. Tell me my son is all right. Tell me I got this place all wrong."

"To golf is to be truly alive, isn't that what you think?" responds LaBelle.

I can't say anything.

"Your son is right here, with you, golfing, Monsieur

Khoury. Aren't you happy about that?" she continues. "Look at where we are."

"I want out." My words hang there for a second, and neither marshal stirs in response. They're unmoved in every way.

"Talk to your son," LaBelle commands.

"No, I'm not doing this and you can't make me."

"You're focused on the wrong thing again, Mr. Khoury," Fiona says. "Talk. To your son."

"Have a good round, gentlemen," LaBelle says, and the whirr of the power cart starts up again.

"I want out!" I scream at them, but the red cart skitters off, leaving us alone on the course.

Payne and I stand there for a minute, watching the cart disappear into the woods. Tears reach the corners of my eyes.

"I don't want to die," Payne says.

I pull him into my arms. I can feel his convulsions against my belly as he weeps, and I scream my anguish into his shoulder until his collar is wet from my breath and tears.

"What if I die alone, Dad?" he whispers into my ear.

"Never. You're never alone, son," I weep into him, but all I can think of is how I have failed Payne. That's why he did this. He lived in our house but we abandoned him, left him in his cave to ward off evils we parents did not fully understand. We were too busy fighting with ourselves and each other. He had no chance.

"We should tee off," I say to Payne. "Because if we don't, I don't know what happens next. But if we do, if we golf together, we get to stay together."

Payne shrugs and relents. I pull a ball out of my pocket: it's the one marked with the greater-than sign again. More math. Something is supposed to add up.

I tee off but don't keep my eye on the ball on the follow-through. I don't follow through at all. Who cares?

"There's this tattoo guy in the Village who doesn't check IDs," Payne volunteers. "Cost me like two hundred bucks."

"You overpaid," I say. "Ball between your feet," I add accidentally as he lines up, like I did a thousand years ago when he was a little boy. Instead of teenage blowback, Payne adjusts his feet. He swings his 7-iron and the ball lofts quite nicely down the middle.

"Oh, hey," he says, pleasantly surprised, and suddenly the smell of the forest returns to my nostrils and the wind rattles through the leaves a bit more loudly, like a reminder that it's there and we are here. A peregrine falcon circles above, spying a future kill. I don't know what hole this is, but it's gorgeous. There's a marsh in front of the undulating green, and behind it sits exposed bedrock encircling the back like a stole. This is the spot where Karl had the talk with me about Krista.

We each clear the marsh, but my ball rolls up on the bedrock and shoots back and left, onto the green. Payne's ball doesn't do what he wants it to do, but he still gets it there. The ball makes a beeline for the flagstick and I can't help but voice my excitement as it gets closer, closer, coming to rest maybe two feet from the hole.

"Real good shot," I tell him. And then I under-hit a lengthy putt. "FISM," I blurt out, then putt again, and burn the lip of the cup. Three putts. Payne cautiously makes his putt to bogey the hole and beat me, soundly. Besting me makes him smile to himself.

I couldn't be happier about it.

"Why do we all do this stuff if we all end up the same way when we're done?" Payne asks. "Life is a fuckin' joke. Or maybe we're all jokes, but with the same punchline."

"I don't think life is funny," I say, and he grunts in agreement.

We walk down the fairway, which looks like it's been laid down with a God-sized paintbrush. Payne walks right beside me. Our pull carts nearly touch wheels.

"I think we do what we do because we need to feel like it's not just preordained, you know?" I say. "Like we have a choice in the sequence of events."

"Do we though?"

"I think we do."

"How many times you play the fifth hole after the sixth hole?"

That is a question I've never asked myself.

"Life is just a series of steps," Payne says to me. "It doesn't progress. It's like a dot-to-dot picture; one thing leads to another, and then it ends. And nobody says anything about it."

"*Things progressed*," *I admit to Karl. "I don't know how one thing leads to another.*"

"*Get it right*," *Karl tells me. "It's a stink on the both of you now.*"

"What club do I hit?" Payne asks, and I'm happy to advise.

"We probably have four hundred yards to go, so the

longest one you're comfortable with. See that blue stick way down there? Blue is two. Two hundred yards to the green from that stick."

He pulls out a 7-iron. "I know I can hit this one." I shrug and let him use it without complaining. As he lines the shot up, Payne says, "You know, maybe we all need some kind of sequence in our lives, like a process where we know that there are steps to follow. If you know there's a next step in the sequence maybe that makes this step easier to get through."

That idea strikes me somewhere deep. I never thought about golf as a process; a sequential challenge that gives a player hope that there might be order in the world and a linear reason for living.

"Payne, you're a genius," I say to him.

He fires the 7-iron straight into the woods.

"Nice shot," I tell him.

We golf, father and son, not worrying about how well the shots go, and a warmth grows between us; the hostility melts away, and I offer him gentle advice every time he asks for it, with no criticism or disappointment. We are both present through this sequence of eighth hole to ninth hole and into the back nine.

I try not to let my mind linger in dark places for too long.

"Hey," I tell my boy. "I know you hate this."

"I hate golf, but I love you, Dad. This is what you like. I can like it."

We're far away from the clubhouse. I think we're maybe on the eleventh hole. Payne has trouble with his swing that he can't seem to correct. By the time he gets to the green, he's reached double-par.

Payne says, "Instead of wondering what I'm doing here, maybe we should be wondering what you're doing here."

"We're all heroes of our own stories, right?"

He looks into my eyes pensively. It makes me uneasy. I bend to focus on my putt. As I stare at the > marking, I whisper, "You can tell me it's a gimme from here."

"Nice try," he whispers back and we both smile to ourselves.

The round may have lasted four and a half hours or four and a half minutes. But the clubhouse is in our sights, and so is the practice green, past the flag of the eighteenth hole. The end of this sequence is in sight.

Payne looks to me as we sidle up to our approach shots. "Dad?"

"Yes, Payne?"

"You think we can live non-sequentially? Like, can we not know what the next step is going to be and still be okay with it?"

"Oh, for sure," I lie to him. Not that I believe we can't, but I don't know the answer. I think about what the next step is, after we manage to get ourselves onto the green, then urge our way into the hole, then shake hands—a father and son congratulating each other for finishing the sequence. And after the handshake, I'll find myself on another golf course and Payne will be banished somewhere for eternity. I'm not okay with that.

I step up to my ball and Payne follows me, standing way too close to a person who's about to swing a club. "Whoa,"

I say before he slides his arms around my neck and brings me in for a hug.

I melt into his chest. Payne comforts me.

"Something has to happen after this, Dad, and I'm okay with whatever that is. I don't need to know what's next."

I push away. "No," I tell him. "I'm not going gently. If there's a way to bring you back, I'm bringing you back. I'm going to fight."

The red marshal's cart comes flying out from behind the clubhouse.

"You made it angry," Payne says, and I can see LaBelle's glare from twenty yards away. Suddenly, everything green gives way to black again before I can tell my boy goodbye.

"I hate this stupid game," Payne says to me as he trudges toward the forest trail that goes back to our cottage. The lights on his tiny shoes blink whimsically with every step he takes, betraying his temper tantrum.

"Payne, get back here," I tell him, and he complies. Junior golf is only a dollar at Victoria Beach Golf Course on Tuesdays, so it's not like I'm worried about losing a dollar. Junior Day means I get my boy to play this agonizing, deifying, life-defying game, even if he doesn't love it yet.

I tell him to point his nose down at the ball, right at the pink heart that Faith has drawn on it. I wrap my arms around his and we make a pendulum motion together. After three or four tries, he makes contact and the ball skitters maybe twenty yards along the ground.

He beams up at me with pure six-year-old glee. He has conquered the forces of nature. He has fallen for golf, I think.

I will never be happier.

11

VICTORIA BEACH, 2011

I love that there are no tee times at Victoria Beach. You show up and drop your ball in the top of a tubular metal device that looks like two prongs of a white pitchfork, and once the ball reaches the bottom, you're up. A sign beneath the device reads:

2ND ROUND 1ST ROUND
SECOND ROUND SHALL
ALTERNATE WITH FIRST

On Sunday mornings especially, this device has probably saved the staff from many a conflict. I tend to stick to the evenings, when it's more likely to golf without making new acquaintances.

People sometimes golf barefoot here. Sandals are

common. Beneath the grass is beach sand, which makes the course extremely walkable. It also kills any roll your ball might have, which can take some adjusting to if you've come from a cheap muni course with hardened riverbank clay as its underlying soil.

I have this eerie instinct that I've been here before, and I know from having looked it up that I often experience what is known as *déjà vécu,* which means "having lived through already." It's not quite your classic déjà vu, where an experience seems familiar. Instead, something happens, and I think, "Yes, that's happened before, and then ..." and then the next thing happens, and I think, "That's what happened last time too!"

Could it all be tied together? This déjà vécu ... my memory jumble ... eternal golf courses?

The evening sun is casting its final rays on Victoria Beach Golf Course. I try to disregard the déjà vécu feeling, telling myself I've been out on this course at this time, as the sun sets, a hundred times. *It's familiarity you're feeling,* I tell myself. A memory twitch. But I know it's something more.

The clubhouse attendant—the one person who operates the whole course—is gone for the night. Is it LaBelle? Whoever it was, they've put up the blue and white sign that says, "We will return at," and an adjustable clock indicates 7:00 a.m. I have definitely walked from the trail in the woods, into the clubhouse clearing, past the clock sign, but every ray of orange sunlight and every leaf that falls has happened before.

I examine the white, tubular pitchfork that holds golf balls and keeps the sequence of players in order.

There's one ball at the bottom of the tube. My ball. With a big, green number seven on it, written by someone I never met because it was a found ball.

I just got here.

I half expect to see myself walk out from around the corner. Maybe I'm taking a whizz in the bushes, because the outhouse would be locked up after hours. And then reason kicks in, and I deduce that someone has found my lost number seven ball and left it here, in the off chance the rightful owner finds it. This does occasionally happen to a found golf ball, so long as it isn't worth anything. It gets left behind in case it doesn't hold intentions well. No one wants one of those.

What would I say if I saw myself walking out from the bushes and my playing partner was me?

"We all make mistakes," I'd say. I chuckle and think unlimited mulligans would be wise to suggest. I'd like a mulligan on a lot of things in life, and if I was standing right in front of another version of me, right now, tasked with giving him some kind of profound insight to send him into the Beyond, I have no idea what I'd say or think. There is no answer. I'm lost.

Right on cue, my back starts acting up before I even reach for a golf club, like it did the time I already lived through here at Victoria Beach, and suddenly the déjà vécu kicks in with all-encompassing force. I know what's going to happen next:

I'm going to tee off here and heel the ball so badly it will roll like a dead duck into the tall grass on the left, leaving me with a two-hundred-and-fifty-yard shot from the rough. Then Faith will walk out of the forest behind the golf course with her cart as I'm taking the steps down from the tee box. She'll look sad, but I won't say anything about that. I'll be too thrilled that she's here, that she decided to golf with me in the face of what golfing means to her now.

I'll say, "Hi, babe," and she'll stand solemnly at the red tees like she's lining up for a firing squad. She'll swing her pink driver carefully and with too much control, and she'll shrug at her straight, short tee shot. "Good start," I'll say to her, and she'll thank me cordially, and we'll quietly play our last round of golf together, ever.

Neither of us will talk about Chi-Chi and how impossibly difficult it is for her to be golfing right now.

She'll try to not think about it, at first, how every time she touches a golf club it's both a tribute and dirge. But any attempt at pleasantry will depart by the end of the gargantuan par-5 second hole. Neither of us will keep track of how many shots it takes her to get onto the second green, and I will offer a number we both know is charitably low. She'll take a snowman, because we've agreed that her maximum is three over par, per hole. We shouldn't even be keeping score.

We'll cut through the thick patch of forest along a hundred-year-old path that gets you to the hidden par-3 third. I'll think, This is the opposite of fun, being here with all the pain sitting on our shoulders, *but I won't speak as we both have a miserable time up and down the undulations of the sloping green. I won't mark my putts, because I only have Chi-Chi's dime to mark them with, and I don't know what Faith will think of that.*

On the fourth, which gently doglegs to the left, there is a large, mature shrubbery to the right Faith and I have affectionately nicknamed "The Ball-Eating Bush." The running joke will end as Faith lines her feet up wrong and hits a perfectly straight drive right into the bush. Neither of us will see a ball emerge, but we won't laugh at the joke. Faith's face will harden and her shoulders will slope lower—not with anger at the mistake, but like igneous rock, she will petrify.

As we walk, single file, down the long, forested path between the end of the fourth and the nestled tee box of the fifth, I will think about stopping to turn and say something to Faith. To tell her we each need some help from someone to deal with all of this. I could break the whole thing open and exclaim that she's suffering from something that could quite justifiably be called "depression" if we were to agree that it was helpful to apply such a label. I might also be labelled with the same affliction. It might be the labelling that would help us not feel this way anymore, as though we were a couple of mountains submerged in the same ocean that declared themselves volcanoes. We could make an island out of all these continental rifts and subductions.

But I won't stop walking. Faith will offer some small talk: "No bugs." I will agree. It's autumn and Chi-Chi is dead; both things that I will leave hanging in the silence.

On the sixth, I'll ruminate about leaves and leaving. I will lose my ball to the left, and Faith will lose hers to the right. I'll get so deeply lost in thought she'll need to scream at me to hurry up and take a drop. Something will bubble up in her, but it's malformed. Her ball will roll along the downslope of the fairway and up to the green, and she will be five feet from the hole, having nailed a green from more than a hundred and fifty yards away. Instead of leaping for joy or seeking my congratulations, she'll hunch over as she pulls her cart. She'll look angry that she has to walk so far without taking a break for a shot.

We'll park our clubs behind the berm that separates the sixth and seventh, and we'll eschew the forest path to walk up the seventh fairway, drivers in hand. I will fall down the parasitic cone of golfing denial I have created and tell her that she's golfing well, that it's fun to be out here with her. She'll look down at her shoes so hard that she will almost start to slowly implode, her eyes being the first to fall inside of her. We will be so far gone and I won't be able to admit it. Not until I see it for a second time.

The seventh has a lone oak tree standing in middle, and if you know what's good for you, you'll aim for it, because the best way to miss a hazard (or any target) on the golf course is to aim for it. I guess when you intend the unintended consequences, they no longer become unintended. I will consider this as we duff our way past the tree. I decide to say something to Faith with the intention of creating unintended consequences. I will ask her what Chi-Chi would have thought of this course, if we had ever asked him to come golfing here. That's the tree I had been golfing around the entire day, and so I will decide to aim right for it, knowing that will ensure that I miss it.

Except I won't miss. I will hit Faith right in the heart, and she will turn to me and explode in my face, tearlessly.

"You neve r... would have let me ... invite him here," she will say, drawing the sentence out like a growl. She is right, which will make everything grow cold and hard again. As much as I love Chi-Chi and Dorothy, Victoria Beach was our place. It was a place for me to be with Faith and Payne, where they would be all mine. I will laugh at myself for thinking that, but it will always be true, even if Payne won't come anymore and Faith will never golf with me again.

Faith will finish the seventh hole with another three-over-par, and I will wait for her to sink her ball before I attempt a birdie putt. I will be excited about the possibility of it, and I will lip it out before tapping in for par, and only after seeing this again, after this déjà vécu, will I see how I was stupidly focused on scoring, instead of making amends. I will think that this hole always gets my goat, and how I need to spend more time reading greens. What a selfish asshole I will be.

Am.

The eighth will be the longest hole on the course, despite being a two-hundred-yard par-3 with only one obstacle (a pine sapling), because Faith will fire her ball into the leaves and then stand like a statue, her arms limp, her eyes vacant, and she'll stare into the woods and murmur, "I don't think I can do this anymore," and I'll get annoyed.

"Come on," I'll urge her, "there's one hole left after this," and I'll keep on golfing, because I love it. I'll hit the green and get even more annoyed that she doesn't care about how I made a good shot. I'll slide my hybrid back into the bag and look up at her, pretending I didn't realize she's been motionless all along.

"Honey," I'll say to her, in that way that drips with resentment and disinterest; a way only someone who truly loves you can say it. "Honey," I'll say again, and the tone of it makes me hate myself. Only now do I see how cruel I'll be in that moment, with that word so sour.

Faith will shudder at the taste of it. "I can't," she'll say, and only in this déjà vécu will I feel her without feeling myself. She's not talking about golf. This is the moment where we fell apart. I was so hopeful we could play together forever.

I won't go up to her and caress her cheek and tell her it's okay. I won't bring her into my arms and squeeze the pain out until she can bear it. I won't drive my club into the turf like it's a sword and proclaim my fealty to her, to us, to anything. I won't defend the marriage we've built. I won't tell her Chi-Chi broke my heart too, or that we're a couple of shattered plates trying to clean each other up and it's impossible. Nope.

She will tell me, "If you're interested in someone else, admit it so we can end this."

I will draw my putter from its holster and proclaim, "I'll give you bogey on the next two if you don't want to play. Will you walk with me at least?"

Faith will shrug. I will walk around to her pull cart and bring it to her so she can get moving. I'll get close enough to touch her hand, to place her head on my clavicle and stroke her hair, to say something comforting, but I won't do it.

Thankfully, Faith will start to move toward the green like a steam locomotive, and all the tension in my shoulders and neck will ease enough for me to focus on the birdie putt, as though it were my greatest achievement, while our marriage sheds itself from us like a jackknifing semi-trailer rolling on the Coquihalla Highway. I won't see it happening because I won't look back. Faith will never golf with me again. The world we built will never be the same, not because Chi-Chi died, but because I won't be enough. My selfishness will ruin everything. And now that I'm some kind of infinite golfer, and I can't do anything about it, now I'd give anything, including my eternal soul, to hold Faith in my embrace and make her see that her husband is there with her. Now that I'm not.

Birdie!

When we get to the ninth, I will ask Faith if she's sure she doesn't want to start again, and she'll refuse. It will feel like I'm hauling a mannequin around with me and I'll get even more annoyed, so when we reach the clearing halfway down the fairway, Faith will say she's going back to the cottage and she'll skulk off, and I'll think, Whatever, *and I'll golf alone forever. I will stand at the top of the ninth green and scan everywhere to see where Faith is going. She'll be long gone, but I'll look out for her, hoping she'll come back. She won't.*

We'll spend more than a year adrift in the streams, all three of us. Intentionless. Backspinning.

PAR: 35   SCORE: 42

I see the white metal tee-time device and have another déjà vécu of considering whether to play a second nine that day. I remember looking at this contraption on that day and deciding the lineup was too long to get another nine in. But right now, the metal apparatus sits empty.

Then, from behind the shack where people store their golf clubs, I appear.

This isn't a vision—this is me. I am flesh, right before my own eyes.

My second self walks up to the white contraption, oblivious to the fact that I am here watching him, and drops golf ball after golf ball down the metal chute. Five of them in total.

I recognize the balls as he stacks them on top of each other:

—the three at the bottom of the pile; **3**

—followed by the greater-than sign; **>**

—the barbell; **⊢**

—the green seven; **7**

—and finally, at the top, the three dots. **∴**

And then the other James Khoury looks directly at me, expectantly, and I see what he wants me to understand: a message from myself to myself, peppered through the green purgatory of golf courses, and I understand. I nod to him, and we agree that I must fight to get out of whatever this is, that I must find a way to live, to save my family (if that's even possible), and face all of it head-on instead of golfing as a form of escape. Instead of trying to place my intentions inside of a hunk of rubber and resin made the same colour as the Pope.

The other James Khoury blinks out of existence, then back in for a split second, then gone again, as if he had been unplugged from this reality, like someone pulled the cable.

I let the stream wash over me, turning everything blue, including me.

Faith enters from the kitchen, and I don't know how long I've been here without her. I'm asleep and awake at the same time, like in a daydream. I am so cold.

"Here," Faith says, and she drapes something, carefully, until all of my body is beneath it.

A quilt.

I wrap the quilt tighter around my shoulders and close

*my eyes. The fabric is such a comfort ... a comfort I will
never deserve. I bring the quilt in close and hold it tight.
I look up at her. Her wry smile is no longer part of her
body.*

"I've been true," I tell her.

"Okay," she says.

I curl up tight, like a snail.

"Stop now," a voice calls from behind me and I am
back on the course. LaBelle emerges from the closed-up
clubhouse of Victoria Beach. "What's happening here?"
Suddenly, I've been caught doing something wrong.

"Please calm down, Monsieur Khoury," LaBelle says,
her accent placing the emphasis on the end of my name.

LaBelle looks down at the golf balls, forming the
message that brought her out here. "Who did this?" she
demands.

"I did."

She looks puzzled.

"Another me," I say, and she scowls even harder.

"This won't do."

"You're right," I tell her. "I'm done with this nightmare.
Let me go."

"It's not as easy as letting go. If we let go, it's more than
golf that will end."

She mumbles something to herself in French that I
can't make out. She studies the message. From top to bottom, in the chute, it reads: ∴ LIVE. *Therefore, live.* She shakes
her head and peers back at me, like I am responsible for this
misbehaviour; this unauthorized influence over natural law.

I puff up my chest, certain in my reading of this message. I have a choice. *Do the math. Live.*

We engage in a stare-down. It's almost as though this is LaBelle's job, and I know I am getting in her way. Maybe being a pain in her ass will get me off of the golf course.

"*Un instant,*" LaBelle says, and then she skulks off, muttering French curses under her breath.

I'm coming, Faith, I think. *I'm going to fix this. And then, together, we'll rescue Payne.*

But nothing is fixed. Nothing at all.

The black closes in, perhaps because of LaBelle operating behind some kind of curtain. The darkness moves slowly enough for me to see it happening and shout my protests. But it closes in all the same, and twilight falls on Victoria Beach. I turn to run from the blackness but that only makes it come closer. I zig and zag and shield my head, but it doesn't matter. There's a lightning bolt of anguish that starts in the back of my hip and rockets up and down the back of my body. My body spasms and I fall into the creeping twilight, leaving Victoria Beach behind.

Everything goes dark.

And then the light switch goes on. A flare of terrifying memory.

It's after midnight. It's the mother of all fights.

The picture frames rattle on the cottage walls. The neighbouring cottagers can hear us, for sure. Everybody's walls are paper-thin. We might end up on the Victoria Beach community Facebook page.

I'm afraid she'll leave forever, she's so angry. She pounds the bedroom door with her fist before she lays into me again.

"How am I supposed to move on if you're always there to remind me about how I fail? Fail as a wife? Fail as a mother?"

"I don't think that."

"Oh, you do. You keep score. You count every single goddamn item."

"Not true."

"Isn't it? How many times did you give me one of those
finger-lists of yours? 'All the ways Faith fails James'?"

"Come on."

"How many times? You totally keep score."

She quiets down.

"It's a game I can't win, James. I'm not playing it anymore."

"Please don't leave. Not now." I let gravity lead me onto
the bed.

She's at the doorway when I blurt, "Aren't you gonna ask
me about my appointment this morning?"

"Ah," she says. "Yet another failure on my part." And then
the doorway empties.

12

LE GÉANT, 2018
Québec: Eighteen Holes
Thomas McBroom

The stage lights come on, which instantly gives me a headache, but it allows me to see the stage: Mont-Tremblant. The memory makes me groan. I got two shirts in one day when I was here last; one shirt from each of the two courses, but they were consolation prizes for how terrible the day turned out to be.

I'm on a mountain sequence designed by Thomas McBroom. This was the place where I closed the biggest deal of my career with a modular home manufacturer named Truong who was so infatuated with golf he wanted to play both Le Géant and Le Diable, all in one day. It's a cold autumn day in the Laurentians, with a dusting of snow threatening to stay put, despite the white sunlight blanketing everything. It won't be long before people are skiing around here.

I am so cold. A special kind of bone-cold. That kind of cold where, even if you had a blanket, or someone to cuddle, it would still frost your marrow.

I don't have the energy to golf for eight hours.

The pain is here too, rekindling in every receptor.

Now, more than ever, I need my quilt.

It's all becoming clear. Golf isn't a cancer that slips into your cerebrospinal fluid; this is *literally* cancer, and the leptomeningeal disease makes my memory short-circuit, from past to future and through and around—that's what got into me. My memory is sick. I am sick. All of this is a fever dream; a death dream. A golf dream.

I haven't forgotten the message I left for myself at Victoria Beach. Even when golf gives me complete acceptance, and even joy, it doesn't put my family back together the way I want it to.

They're not here. I'm in the clubhouse at Le Géant, a quarter of the way through a miserable day in paradise.

Krista is here. We're getting hot toddies at the bar, tucked away from the surely suspicious eyes of our playing partners.

Krista sticks her hands out. They're rosy from the cold. "Feel me."

"Krista."

She motions with her hands. "Come on. Warm them up. I'm freezing."

"Krista, stop. I'm your boss."

She withdraws her hands like she's been stung. I've never said anything about her forwardness before. Until now, I let it happen. Krista looks confused.

I turn to the bar to pick up our drinks. From behind me, she slides her hands into my front pockets.

"That's better," she says.

"Stop," I tell her, but my hands are full. I've also never told her to stop before. I try to twist out of her arms and check around for witnesses, although I'm not sure if I'm scanning to ease my conscience or to see if anyone can help me. I have to ask her to stop a second time before I can pull myself away. It's an awkward wrestle.

"Seriously?" She eyes me for a second, surprised by my reaction. "What, so now you want to be all holier-than-thou?"

"I love my wife."

"But we're not doing anything. We're playing. I thought you were up for playing, blowing off some steam. It's all fun."

"Of course it's not fun. It's far more than that. It's … golf."

Krista runs her hand through her bangs. She's peeved but tries to hide it.

"We should get back," she says. "I'm going to close this deal with Truong and you're going to give me the whole commission. And then I'd appreciate it if you talked to Karl about finding me somewhere else to work."

"Karl knows."

Krista bristles when I say it. "Knows what?"

"Somebody told him something. Maybe it was Rhodesy."

"Who the hell is Rhodesy?"

My temples feel like they're being crushed. Head attack. Krista heads for the clubhouse door but I speed up to follow.

"Rhodes? On our team? We golfed with him and Darryl at Tobiano?"

Krista holds the door open and looks at me as I walk through. Looks at me like I have completely lost my mind. She has no idea who Rhodes is.

The headache gets worse. *Did Rhodesy not work with us? How do I know Rhodesy?*

I emerge from the clubhouse and the cold sun blinds me for an instant. Truong sits there in his cart, waiting for us to suffer for his pleasure for twenty-seven more holes.

The world seems blurred around the edges. Balance is something that requires conscious effort. I nearly fall into the cart, slopping the drinks onto my lap.

Krista undoes the strap around her bag. "I'll switch carts," she says to me.

I'm not sure I can drive myself around. I can't play through, or play along. This isn't living. If I had a choice, I'd ditch my clubs right here and I'd be on the next plane home.

Truong has the honour on the tenth hole's elevated tee. We overlook a hole that seems cut right out of Laurentian mountain rock, descending and contoured. A sequence of three petite bunkers runs along the right, like three mathematical markings. The challenge is laid out, verdant and beckoning. A part of me hears the siren call to golf it.

"Stop!" I yell, and Truong twists back to look at me. I fumble and bumble my way out of the cart and to my feet. I scream at the sky, as though it hides some kind of secret observation deck or control room. Or God. "Come out from wherever you're hiding and face me! You'll have to pull the plug on me, every single time, so you might as well come on out and deal with it now. I want to live! No more golf. You hear me?"

This time, my handlers aren't disguised as marshals or caddies.

I walk up to Rhodes. "I'm done with all of this. I don't know why you're here, but if you're in charge, I want out."

"I make the decisions," Fiona says to me from beyond Rhodes's shoulder. He turns back and steps away, deferring to her. There's something dark and sinister in Fiona's face; maybe it's the sunlight casting her features in shadow.

"I will sit down and never move," I tell Fiona. "If that doesn't work, I will walk off-course. If you stop me, I will break every shaft over people's fucking heads. Do you get it? I won't cooperate. Give me my wife and son back."

Fiona looks at LaBelle. LaBelle gives her a look of exasperation.

"It doesn't work that way, Mr. Khoury," Fiona says.

"I don't care," I tell her. My eyes are going to explode. I don't see Truong and Krista anywhere; they've disappeared.

"I'll never quit." I tell Fiona. "I'll be the biggest pain in your ass for however long I have left."

Being this resolute doesn't sway Fiona enough for her to say anything, so I soften my tone.

"I know I'm sick, but I need to get back out there. I left so many divots in my life. I want to repair them before I'm done."

"How about this," Rhodes says to Fiona. "A skins game. Like with his brother. If he wins, he goes back. If he loses, he stays here, full cooperation, no more fighting. He plays it out like he's supposed to."

"A skins game," I announce. "Full cooperation if I lose. But if I win ... wait, who do I play?"

Fiona and LaBelle look at each other again. Finally, LaBelle nods ever so slightly.

"You're a hell of a fighter, but a terrible golfer, b'y. You won't win," Fiona says.

Immediately, the game for my life begins, and where else but at the Thomas McBroom course closest to home.

13

SOUTHWOOD, 2020
Manitoba: Eighteen Holes
Thomas McBroom

On the southern edge of Winnipeg, in the bedroom community of St. Norbert, there are contemplative grounds that were once used by Trappist monks. McBroom took those lands and created narrow, arcing alleys of rolling hills nestled in impossible thatches of reeds and fescue. Hazards abound, strewn across the course like a spike belt. When I played Southwood, I sped over it like a drunk driver. Gleeful from the easing of COVID-19 restrictions, my friend Brady invited me here to play a socially-distanced round with him and his parents, who were members. It started off well enough, with a short but safe drive onto the most forgiving fairway on the course.

Southwood Golf and Country Club then proceeded to absolutely dismantle me. I became so distracted and distraught that I even left a golf club behind—a brand new 8-iron I set down on the fringe of a green. Brady's father had to break his social-distance bubble and drive me back through the course at dusk, trying to find this club, but it was gone. In the clubhouse, I sat near (but not too near) Brady's parents and their country club friends, trying to mask the awkward look on my face, all the while wondering how I was going to tell Faith that I needed to find the money to buy a new set of irons, because they don't sell 8-irons by themselves. Brady suggested that I call the pro shop the next day to see if it turned up, and everyone around the table reassured me that it would happen, but I thought there was no chance.

Luck was on my side though, and the next day I found myself driving to St. Norbert, past the southern tip of Winnipeg, through lady-beetle-infested farmers' fields and into the monastery ruins to recover my blade.

I remember having an egomaniacal reverie about monks as I drove up. I felt like maybe I was a monk myself. I had become monastic in my pursuit of golfing excellence. I tried to perfect my swing mechanics with regular practice, begging for more control over the ball; I was often silent in my supplication, but humbly worked on controlling physics and natural laws. Mostly I was golfing because there were devils outside the temple, and those devils were stronger than me, so the best I could do was to stay inside my holy domain.

Suggesting I did it humbly, in some type of ascetic genuflection, could not have been more egotistical. It was all about me. I see that now. I was in pain and afraid and golf was my hiding place.

This time around, no one is at Southwood, which never happens. There are usually dozens of people at the driving range, chipping green, and separate putting green. There's a hustle and bustle on a summer day, typically, and I appear to have been transported to a blistering July afternoon. The sun makes it difficult to look upward at all, and the bugs have been baked into the grass.

Rhodes pores over his bag, inspecting its contents, while LaBelle performs a violent twist exercise, her driver threaded through her arms. Fiona slips on her glove beside me.

"Eighteen holes," Fiona pronounces. "Every hole is worth exactly one skin. No side bets, no frills or gimmicks. You need to have the most skins after eighteen holes to win this game."

"Wait," I say to her, "this isn't fair. You guys can work together to make sure I lose."

"He's right," Rhodes calls out.

"So what?" LaBelle says.

Fiona chews her lip for a second. "Here's what we're going to do. We're going to give you a chance to escape by playing golf. That's more than most folks get. No one is going to cheat you. How sad for you to feel cheated."

"How can I be sure?" I ask her.

LaBelle throws me a threatening smile. "You're going to have to do something you don't do well, Monsieur Khoury. You're going to have to trust."

"Just play your game," Rhodes reassures me. "I hope you remember those lessons I gave you. You're gonna need 'em."

There are five different colours of tee boxes at each

hole here. The nearest is gold, followed by green, white, blue, and black. Fiona and LaBelle set up at the greens, some fifty yards ahead of Rhodes and me at the blues. It's not until I set up at the tee that the stark contrast of the straw-yellow rough and plush green of the fairways strikes me. There is no flat place anywhere at Southwood; it's as though the golf course is an emerald carpet laid on top of Hot Wheels cars. It's still prairie, but the drama has been heightened by the architect.

Rhodes gives me the honour and so I tee off first. This hole is a trap: it gives you a fat square of fairway to land on, but you're still two hundred and sixty yards from the green, maybe more. For a par-4, you're going to be looking at two shots before you get the putter out, and factoring in two putts, that's a bogey. If you hit the easy landing strip on the first hole, you're not winning any skins.

I select the driver and look at the black-and-white-striped pole, probably five feet tall, stuck in the centre of the fairway and off to our left.

"How far do you think that is?" I ask Rhodes, and he doesn't think long before he offers a response.

"Two-seventy-five, maybe?"

I know I can't get that far. I decide to try a draw, closing my club face and coming at the tee with a low, inside-to-outside swing. I aim a bit to the right and tell the ball—the one marked with three dots—to start right and curve to the left, back to the fairway.

It works. I put all of my back and shoulders into it and my shoulders drop straight down. Imbued with all of my intentions to get back home, to get back to Faith and Payne and my own life and restart everything, that fucking ball drops down on the sloping right edge of the fairway and rolls left for me, closer and closer to the black-and-white yardage marker, almost right up to it like a terrier obeying its master. The drive stops a few yards short, and I figure I landed a two-hundred-and-sixty-yard draw with my driver and have a 9-iron left to get on the green. I've given myself a chance to win this hole. It might be the greatest shot I've ever played.

Rhodes lays up. He pulls out the three-wood and swings that light, easy, Gary Player/PGA logo swing, stroking the ball effortlessly with a low line drive that runs up the centre of the fairway and finishes left. He's behind me by about six feet. It's like he took a shortcut.

Fiona, from fifty yards ahead of us, looks back and offers us a thumbs up. She coughs up a high, slicing drive that heads for the reeds to the right. The backspin keeps her ball from rolling that far, and gravity runs it down between two berms on the right-hand side, into the grassy rough. A near disaster.

LaBelle stretches her shoulders like she's about to do a power lift. Her backswing is agonizingly slow, but her swing is Olympic fast. With the fifty yard advantage, LaBelle rolls past my drive with ease. She moves her head from side to side, stretching her neck. I realize my own neck is getting stiff.

"The second shots make or break you on this one," Rhodes says.

Fiona is nowhere near the green with her second. She flops to safety with a wedge, but the fairway is too narrow and she rolls it onto the left fairway, still a hundred yards out.

Rhodes, using a pitching wedge, takes a massive divot

and skies it. He's safe, but he's short of the green, landing on the narrowest strip of runway. A chip shot awaits him next.

Faith loved chip shots. There was something gentle and precise about them, and she was good at them. She chipped in a couple at Victoria Beach over the years, and nothing made a day better than watching her kick up her heels in joyful surprise, and then watching her try to contain her glee because glee isn't appropriate golf etiquette. At a course that permits barefoot golf, cut-offs, sixsomes, and Bluetooth speakers, her need to restrain herself was adorably silly.

My eyes are looking in the direction of the flag but all I can see is the cut of Faith's perfect jaw, her flowing hair in my hand. The light in her crystalline eyes at full celestial sparkle. The Faith of the past.

I need to win this game.

I'm focused on the wrong thing, like Fiona told me, and bring my attention back to the present. I consider the flag instead of longing for my wife. If I aim slightly past the flag, I should be safely on the green. The pin is at the bottom of a low-lying area within the green, so I might even get a good roll. I expel some air and waggle, making sure I'm settled in and my back is as relaxed as I can make it, given the soreness that's starting to build up from my neck downward.

When the ball is hit with the correct contact and high enough speed, it's like you are crushing an eggshell. It feels like nothing. And that's when you know it's going to be good.

My shot feels like a spoon tapping against a hard-boiled

egg, which is almost the feeling I'm looking for, but not quite. I watch the ball's flight silently as it travels, trying to guide it to the target with my body language. It doesn't land on the green at all; instead, it hits the back left fringe, then spins back and rolls onto the green. I've got a twenty-foot downhill putt in my future.

LaBelle sculls her ball, making it shoot low and roll, bounding a few times before making its way to the left bunker. The sand traps here are deep and authentic; she'll be lucky to simply get the ball out and on the green.

I'm the only one who's on in two. Using a 9-iron, Rhodes chips with precision. His ball lands on the front-most edge of the green and rolls as far as it flew, down into the depression where the flag rests, but past the hole. It comes to a halt a good twelve feet from the pin.

LaBelle stands in the sand trap with her leading left leg well above her right. She tries to flex her left knee to even it out, but she looks awkward, and her face registers annoyance that she needs to even try this shot. She barrels into the sand trap with all her might, and an eruption of white sand shrouds her. From somewhere in that wave of sand, her ball emerges, muscled out of the bunker. It flies straight up, narrowly missing the punitive lip at the edge of the trap, and then straight down, short of the green by a foot. "*Crisse de calvaire tabarnak,*" LaBelle mutters to herself.

She powers her ball through the thick Bermuda grass onto the Kentucky Blue with such brutality that the ball scoots into the crater but half-pipes it on the right-hand side, then wheels left. She walks up to her ball, deliberately and carefully, picks it up, and hurls it into the tall grass on our right. She places her head in her hand and urges Fiona with a brusque gesture to take her shot.

From the fringe, Fiona putts down into the depression as well, but her putt breaks too much from the right to left. Not only is she short by three feet, but the break carries her another foot away. It's no gimme from there.

At this point, we've all worked our way down into the depression to make our putts. I hate the word "depression": it's a label, and once you label something, you put it in a jar. It can't breathe. It can't fly. It can't grow. Depression is the jar that kept me from being whatever the hell I was trying to be, for so many years. And then as Payne grew up and became more and more sullen, my greatest fear was that, like a virus or genetic deficiency, I was going to pass my problems along to him, and he'd end up in the jar too. Unable to talk. Deprived of energy. Hating himself. Trapped in a spiral of pessimism, then making things seem worse than they are, then feeling that too.

I had a therapist once tell me that even if your problems are biological and beyond your control, it's better to believe that you have a choice, and I agree with her. That way, even if you're deluding yourself, you're deluding yourself in positive ways. You do have a choice. Your intention matters. I held that close, and I hold onto it still: the vast majority of people can spiral upward. I can believe things are better than they are, and then feel how good they are. It's a matter of telling myself to see it that way, against my own instincts. Faith told me that I was telling my brain to disconnect from my heart. Maybe she's right, but it works.

So I tried to tell Payne about my beliefs, but it all came

out wrong. He told me to treat him like an adult, and so I did. I told him about all the kinds of issues he might some-day suffer from because of me, and pitfalls to avoid that I didn't. I told him how "depression" and all those other labels trap you. Even if they're true, they don't do you any good.

I couldn't stop him from becoming a teenager. The silence and division between us was a force as unassail-able as gravity, inertia, or death. When Chi-Chi died, I put Faith in the jar. Or maybe she put herself there, I can't say. But I need to set her free.

Even if the three of us crazies end up locked in silent resentment, we should be together. And that's why I fight. That's why I have to win.

My turn. From inside the depression, I read my putt breaking from left to right, maybe the length of a put-ter's head. I squat to read it as well as I can, which makes my back pain bark at me like a Rottweiler. But it's only pain. I push myself up to a standing position, practise my putting stroke a single time, look down the barrel of the practice stroke to see the cup, and then wiggle my toes. I try to make the white notch at the top of the club face strike through the ball.

My ball starts left, but perhaps not enough, and then it goes rightward, past the cup. "Hang on," I tell it, "hang on." I can tell its path is too far right.

"Come on, ball," Rhodes says to it. That surprises me, but not entirely. Even when we compete with each other, we can hope for the best. Even when it's not the best for you.

There's a hidden break around the cup that I didn't

read, and it brings my ball left in the nick of time. I drain a birdie putt.

Fiona and Rhodes pick up their balls, unable to match the task, and compliment me on a nice putt. LaBelle has her back turned to us before I can even retrieve my ball.

JAMES: 1

The second hole's elevated green and gentle bend to the right don't provide enough challenge for anyone to stand out. Distance is not an issue on this par-3; LaBelle and Rhodes make par while Fiona and I bogey. The skin carries over, making the third worth two skins.

The pond on the third hole invades my line of sight from the right-hand side. If I hit it short, or slice it, my ball is going to end up wet. Thankfully, and with Rhodes's help at Devil's Pulpit, I have enough confidence in my draw to believe I can hit away from the hazard. My drive is a bit short, but makes the fairway.

Rhodes goes next and he bombs one, three hundred yards long, safely rolling down the middle of the fairway and past the bunkers on either side. He's got a pitch shot for his second. "Nice," I tell him, and we walk together up to the green tees as the women tee off.

Fiona nearly hits the black-and-white one-fifty marker with her shot. Her swing mechanics are awkward and abrupt, like so many players you see who have figured out a way to make it work that would only work for them. LaBelle, meanwhile, is the opposite. Perhaps it's the rage in her intention: she wants to annihilate the ball, or perhaps to annihilate me, I'm not sure which. Perhaps it's both. I can hear her tennis-player grunt from here as she attempts to hammer it. Sure enough, the violence imparts way too much sidespin on the ball and it bananas to the right, clearing the water but landing in the tall, golden straw that adorns every boundary of every hole at Southwood. LaBelle swats at the air with her hand and Rhodes whispers to me, "I think that means it's not happening for her on this hole."

"It's somebody else's skin," LaBelle announces, and Rhodes throws a wink at me.

Fiona miscues a three-wood from a hundred and fifty yards out, but it works out fine, flying with such a low trajectory that it rolls up the middle and circles around the flag. Rhodes congratulates her, as do I, but LaBelle beetles along with us, not even stopping to look for her ball as we pass its last known whereabouts.

Swinging a club hurts in new places: the back of my skull; my ankle, calf, and knee; the front of my forehead; my right wrist. Rhodes gives me a look of concern, but I brush it off with an "I'm good" and check to see where my ball ended up: past the back of the green. We walk another football field before we get to Rhodes's drive, and he lobs a shot more softly than he wanted, leaving a twenty-foot uphill putt for birdie. Compliments all around, save for LaBelle, and we make our way to the green.

I am in such pain I can barely walk, but I don't care. I'm getting out of here whether I need to crawl, cheat, or maim. I rub my wrist as I climb the green and get to my ball. I don't crouch to read the break of the green; instead, I track back to the space between the ball and the hole and try to see it from there. Satisfied, I make my putt, pushing the ball a bit and off to the races it goes. I still have eight feet for par.

Rhodes's putt is well-intentioned and well-read, but he's simply too far away and the greens are the vengeful sort; his ball has all the makings of a winner, with good pace and a healthy line, but something unseen pulls it to the left, and then it reaches an apex before rolling back toward him some three feet. Rhodes motions for Fiona to go, to play despite not being away, and I agree. She's got a four-foot putt for birdie and she's perfect. LaBelle is already on her way to the fourth.

FIONA: 2   JAMES: 1

The third hole was merely a warning shot for the fourth, with this five-hundred-yard par-5 playing Mr. Hyde to the previous hole's Dr. Jekyll. Thomas McBroom's sadistic genius is on full display here: again, there's water invading your view from the right, but this time it's much more intrusive, and it's difficult to see the difference in depth from the last hole to this one. Golfers must aim to the left to find safe harbour, unless they can land it on the postage stamp of flat fairway across the moat. There are four hazards on your mind when you approach your tee shot: pond, bunkers on either side, berms that resemble rough—which aim to kick your ball out of bounds—and the ever-present fescue straw creating a flaxen boundary. It's not wheat, but it reminds you of what this land probably once was, or what it could have been.

Fiona has the honour. She clears the water hazard and rolls her shot between the first set of fairway bunkers. The swing isn't pretty and the loft is too low, but she gets the job done. LaBelle swings harder than ever with her tee shot, and this time she connects. The rightward spin isn't too severe, and the curve lands her on the fairway, but the subsequent bounce is hard to the right, and she finds the second cut of green grass. The berm does the rest, kicking her to the right. She ends up against the edge of tall straw.

"I see it," Rhodes says to her with almost no taunt in his voice. LaBelle shrugs.

I'm getting so sore that I'm not sure I can hit a full driver right now. I take out my three-wood and aim for the safe, fat part of the fairway to the left. It lands right in the centre of the fairway, taking the water and bunkers out of play, but I'm way short. The uphill slope kills any forward roll and leaves me with both a good lie and dissatisfaction that I didn't take McBroom's bait and go for it.

Rhodes clears the pair of bunkers that lay in wait for golfers who can't carry the ball two hundred and fifty yards—clears them with ease.

I'm farther back than anyone else. "Two clubs from here," I tell myself.

I reach back and cock my wrists, standing directly above the ball, and I get that soft, sensual contact that is almost erotic when it's right. The ball lofts and gently breaks left, my intentions made whole and real. I step forward a few paces to get to the top of a rolling mound and see that I'm right by the one-fifty marker. That will do.

Fiona and LaBelle each miss the fairway with their second shots, and both end up to the left and short of me.

Looks like Rhodes's hole to lose, and he doesn't disappoint, getting close enough to the green with his second shot to fire an accurate lob wedge straight up and down.

LaBelle smashes the ball past the fairway again, and again she spins on a heel and turns her back on the ball.

"Do you even enjoy golf?" I ask her as she passes.

"*Voyons donc*, joy has nothing to do with this game," she hisses at me.

"Then why even play, LaBelle?" Fiona and Rhodes freeze, looking to LaBelle for her reaction. They're clearly intimidated by her.

LaBelle bares her teeth at me. "I'm here because I took an oath to take care of this, and now it's my duty. My duty to take care of you here."

"Take care of me?"

"*C'est ça.*"

"You sound like a gangster."

LaBelle shrugs and purses her lips with a grim kind of confidence.

"An oath to whom?" I ask her. "The Godfather? Can I talk to him, or her, or whoever's in charge? Is it Thomas McBroom?"

Something ignites inside of LaBelle. I can see it in her eyes as she approaches me. "What makes you think I'm not in charge, Monsieur Khoury? What makes you think I couldn't end this for you right now? We have rules here. Rules you don't want to follow. It's not my job to enforce the rules, but it's my duty to respect them and obey. What happens when you lose, huh? Are you going to respect and obey the rules?"

The truth is, I won't obey until they end me. I will fight until I am no more.

"Can we continue, please?" Fiona calls out, but LaBelle cocks her head to the side and looks deeply into my eyes.

"You won't let go, will you? You think you're in some kind of simulation here, like virtual reality or a vision quest or something. Once this game ends, there will be no more golf. There will be no more blue sky or pleasant grass or gentle breeze or human contact. There will be darkness."

"Purely conjecture," Rhodes says as he steps between LaBelle and me. "Hey, a word for a moment?" he asks LaBelle, but she continues her tirade.

"There will be darkness that covers you like tar, thick and *étouffer*—stifling—so you are like a bug in a black hole for the remainder of eternity."

Rhodes tries to pull LaBelle away from me, but he's too late.

"Stop fooling yourself," she hisses. "You will not get fire. You will not get pearly gates or cottony clouds."

"Enough!" Rhodes barks at her as they back away from me, but LaBelle keeps shouting.

"Once this game is finished, win or lose, the veil rises for you. We're bringing you out of this, fight or no fight!" Rhodes has led her to the tall grass where she struggles to free herself from his grasp.

Fiona has watched all of it from a distance, with both hands on top of her head, like something has gone horribly wrong. She finally shouts something to LaBelle that I can't quite hear, and LaBelle stops fighting. She stands straight, bristling at me like a threatened animal.

Rhodes signals at me with big arm gestures to shoot my ball, and I set up like a robot. This new information buzzes in my mind. I notice I'm hitting the greater-than ball, which is actually a *V* ball, and I think about how LIVE could also be VEIL. Could also be EVIL. I know less about what is happening to me than I ever have.

It's not a 6-iron from one hundred and fifty yards, but I hit one anyway and rocket the shot twenty yards past the green. When I look back up, LaBelle is gone.

Fiona is on in four. Rhodes nails his wedge and he's six feet from the pin with a birdie putt. I tell him to go ahead, Fiona nods, and he drains it.

FIONA: 2   RHODES: 1   JAMES: 1

LaBelle doesn't reappear at the fifth tees. The short par-4 isn't easy by any means, and the fire of my pain has turned into a body-sized throb that travels to my fingers. I sky my first shot straight up into the air and I know I've lost the hole before it comes down, a hundred yards away. I keep playing, but I'm two shots behind by the time I limp to the green.

Rhodes three-putts and Fiona does enough to bogey it as well. The skin carries over.

As we walk to six, I ask Rhodes if LaBelle quit playing. He turns to Fiona for the answer, and she says, "LaBelle got called away. It's just going to be us."

Being a short driver works in my favour on this long par-4. The fairway gets wide enough to land a plane after about two hundred yards, then narrows to the point of choking at around two-sixty; an invitation by McBroom for longer golfers to lay up. Rhodes does exactly that, hitting a three-wood from the tees and parking it in the centre of that fat part of the fairway. I hit my pre-Rhodes stock driver shot: a slicing two-hundred-and-twenty yarder that barely hangs on to the rightmost edge of the fairway, between first and second cuts of grass. Given the amount of pain I'm in, I'm okay with that.

Sixty yards ahead and to the left, Fiona hits a low roller that's probably the same length as my tee shot, but lands her on the narrowest part of the fairway.

I try to take a shortcut, since I'm on the right fairway and the hole bends leftward. I attempt to draw a 5-iron to clear the rough and land directly on the green. There's no room for error; the green is elevated and I'm not working with any fairway at all. It goes horribly wrong. I overswing with too closed of a club face and my ball shoots into the straw.

Rhodes is next and smokes a low line drive with his 5-iron right onto the green. It draws beautifully, right to left as he intended, and the subsequent roll gets him close to the flag. I'm two hundred yards back.

"That's what *I* was trying to do," I call to him.

"Probably should have held the fairway, even if you can't make the green. That was the strong play there, I think."

"Focused on the wrong thing, maybe," Fiona says, and I shrug. They're both probably right.

Fiona's ball is not far from the one-fifty stick, and she manages to take her mechanically awful swing and turn it into a beautiful shot, parking the ball with almost no roll onto the green. We can't see the ball but it must be close.

Rhodes and I both congratulate her as I make my way to the brambles of yellow grass and shrub.

I think about picking my ball up, but that would be quitting. I can't quit. Call it providence or call it a glitch in the simulation, but I had no trouble recovering golf balls in my previous rounds, so in this most important of all golf games, I figured my ball would simply appear, and maybe have some kind of mysterious message from The Designer written on it in permanent marker. It doesn't. I wave Fiona on as I search beneath the auburn-yellow thicket. I keep searching as she takes her shot.

I kick the straw with an increasing sense of futility after the requisite amount of time. "Sorry guys, sorry," I say to Fiona and Rhodes, but I doubt they hear it. I high-step my way through the tall grass and back out to the fairway. I walk backward, back toward my original position when I shot the ball. I try to visualize the shot again from the same perspective.

And that's when it occurs to me, how I recall everything that's ever happened in my life from the same perspective: trying to figure out how I lost things by running back to the originating point and looking at it exactly the same way. *How stupid is that?*

I veer off to the side, right into the middle of the fairway. I try to find a higher vantage point. I walk closer to the landing spot. I go past it. I get even deeper into the rough. I squat. I get on my hands and knees, even though a dull knife twists into the small of my back. Instead of looking at it from the same perspective all over again, I take a step to the side. I press my face down to the clay loam beneath the beachgrass. Suddenly, I'm looking directly at the "therefore" on the surface of my golf ball and I feel the symbol projecting directly into my mind. I understand why Payne doesn't like golf anymore: because of me.

I take a drop and fire a decent gap wedge up and onto the green, but Fiona and Rhodes have each parred the hole. The skin carries over.

The par-5 seventh hole is worth three skins. Running alongside Rue des Trappistes, the hole doesn't feature a significant amount of trouble for the right-handed golfer until the green, where a marsh lays in wait and a bunker lurks behind. It's the bunker that gets Rhodes on his second shot. Fiona plays it safe and gets on the green in four. I take it easy on my driver, partially due to the pain and partially due to my utter lack of confidence in how I'm swinging it right now, and the results are good enough. I'm short with my third shot and chip past the cup with my fourth. I hit a standard two-putt for bogey. Fiona also makes bogey. It's Rhodes's skin to win. His sand wedge shot is fantastic, but leaves him forty feet downhill to make birdie.

"No pressure," he says to me with a grin as he passes by. After a lengthy deliberation, he pushes the ball right and with way too much force, and it races down, eight feet past the hole. "FISM," he says to himself. Rhodes misses his second putt and taps it in, just to hear the sound of the ball in the cup. We each bogey. The skin carries over.

If I can win this eighth hole, I can take control of the game with four more skins and ten holes left. I try to concentrate but the pain is starting to make my knees tremble.

"You okay, James?" Rhodes asks. "Having trouble?"

"It's nothing," I tell him. "I got this. Let's play."

"We can take a break," Fiona offers. "Let's manage the

pain," and Rhodes nods, which I find quite odd, since I haven't said anything about pain at all. I guess I don't hide things as well as I think I do. I shake my head and start warming up with a 7-iron.

Rhodes says, "We can stop and go again when you're feeling better," but I won't hear of it. This little par-3 isn't going to get the best of me. I can hit my 7-iron a hundred and fifty yards, water or no water, crown of bunkers or no crown of bunkers. I come up short but get a lucky bounce to the left, rolling my ball right onto the fringe. My lumbar spine is a ratty cloth that someone is wringing, but I refrain from grabbing it.

"Nice shot," Fiona concedes.

Rhodes sticks a 9-iron right onto the green, cratering the fragile soil beneath the hole with the impact and backspin, sending the ball backward when it lands. "Oh no," he says, but not too plaintively, as the ball rolls away from the flag. It's not up to his standards, but he's in good shape.

We collect our things, me much more slowly than Rhodes. I don't see Fiona's swing but I see the low flight of her ball, and I recognize the sound of impact. She uses a hybrid and it's too much club. Fiona hammers a power draw, but this is the worst possible time for that. She manages to strike the knoll that connects the green and the rearmost bunker. Her ball caroms leftward and disappears into a grove of ancient trees at the edge of the monastic ruins.

I can't help myself. "Focused on the wrong thing?"

She smiles at me with more grace than I expect. "I shouldn't be golfing to win things or lose things. I golf so I can golf," she says.

"So it's kind of a Zen approach for you," I say to her as

we walk. "You golf best when you achieve a meditative golf state."

"What about you, James Khoury? When do you golf best?"

"If I knew that recipe, I'd cook it up every day."

I used to think it was when I managed to find some kind of "zone," like what the high performance athletes talk about on sports documentaries of their greatest achievements. A zone of unconscious communion with pure intention, like you have temporary command over the forces of nature, and as soon as you think about it, you'll no longer have it, so you force everything out of your mind except for the next shot—like golfing is a Magic Eye puzzle, except you're using your third eye. What gets me into the zone? *Everything in life made safe and secure? A happy wife?*

Maybe there's something inside us that can't break free until it's safe to do so. If it was easy to get into the zone, people would get there all the time. There is no recipe. There are maybe some paths that lead you there, but somebody keeps fucking with the signposts on the trail.

"It's not how you golf," I say.

"False," Rhodes retorts as he pulls up along my right side. "Golf is the struggle for perfection, and sometimes you achieve it. Why else would so many people be obsessed with it?"

Perfecting themselves before Nature Herself. The thought appears like a banner pulled by a flaming biplane across the sky of my mind. To golf is to perfect one's self as nature bears *witness.* And maybe that's why it becomes more fun with age. Maybe we all possess some innate desire to perfect ourselves. To prepare ourselves.

Rhodes continues, "You, James. You think your way through every single shot. You're calculating and trying to run through checklists every single time. I've taken care of your type a million times."

"I need to think it through, Rhodesy. Think through the pain."

"You need to let yourself *feel*, James."

We arrive at my ball. It rests on the fringe, leaving me with an extremely tough read: down a slope and then up a slope, all the while tilted from right to left. Rhodes has an excellent chance of making it and taking the four skins.

"Should I even bother?" Fiona asks, and we both shrug. She tosses her hand in the direction of the trees and says, "Let the monks have it," as though monks still live in the monastery ruins. Fiona stands on the knoll, the highest point on this hole, and watches us compete from above.

I'm up first. I need these skins to escape and to be with my family. I try to look at every single portion of this putt's future journey, breaking hard left and fast, then across the bottom of the basin about six feet, then uphill to the cup, but still breaking somewhat left. If I tweak it, the whole journey changes … I need to not think. So I just putt.

I end up missing so badly that I don't even get it uphill enough to be on the same plane as the cup. I've all but handed the skins to Rhodes. I rub my neck and try to loosen the tendons that coil around my atlas vertebra and release the pressure between my spine and the base of my skull. I groan, and only partially because of my terrible shot.

Rhodes's ball runs uphill, breaking ever so gently to the

left, heading straight for the back of the cup and in. But before it gets there, it hops over the tiniest of twigs and bounds right. The ball stops two blades of grass short from the lip of the hole.

"Thought that was going in," Rhodes says, flashing me a playful look of puzzlement. I can tell he's annoyed too. He wanted it.

"Looked good," I reply. "Finish it off." He taps it in and the pressure is on me to sink this.

I think it through. I'm at the bottom of a depression in the green. The hole is at the top. I have to climb five feet uphill and the break is right to left. I figure I need to aim maybe eight inches to the right. I squat down to get a closer look, but I have to lower myself slowly, at a wheelchair lift's pace, and try not to grimace. I try to put the pain out of my mind instead.

Standing up again takes twice as long as squatting. Neither of my opponents says a word, but I can feel them staring into my back.

Use your big muscles. Shoulders and back, not wrists and hands. Don't think about how much pain you're in. Centre of the club face. Out of the depression. Back of the cup. Point at that target with your follow-through. I think as much as I can possibly think.

I get good contact between club face and ball—a squishy feeling—and it rolls without bounding, up and to the right, then comes left as it should, but it's light. It slows before I want it to, slower, slower—*please get there*—and after an eternity, it plunks into the bottom. The sound of that ball hitting the plastic is unlike any other sound in the world, and my response to it is utter Pavlovian pleasure.

Congratulations all around. The skin carries over.

Five skins await the winner of the ninth hole, giving them what must be an insurmountable lead into the back nine. The new, well-appointed clubhouse provides a backdrop for this hole, as though the elevated green is its stage floor. From our tees, we can only see the tip of the clubhouse's rooftop, four hundred yards away. Ancient oaks loom on either side, obstructing our view as much as the change in elevation does. To our left, I can see the limestone façade of the monastery ruins, its empty, circular second-floor window containing nothing but sky. It lurks like a forgotten spectator. The circular emptiness of the window seems to frame the sky itself, as though it had found a better purpose than simply holding on to stained glass or people.

"Big hole," Fiona says, and it takes me a split-second to realize she's talking about the magnitude of winning the ninth, not the hole in the building that lets the heavens through. I nod.

"No pressure," Rhodes says with a chuckle to himself, and I know he is in fact adding pressure by saying that.

Hitting the driver off the tee seems like a risky endeavour. I'm thinking of an easy 4-iron to start the hole and then taking a look at what I have from there. The 4-iron isn't the easiest to hit, so I immediately commence with the mental checklist of adjusting for the club length and making sure I can make solid contact at high speed. *Don't swing hard; swing fast.*

In the meantime, Rhodes goes first and hits a monster drive. His follow-through pulls his body to the left violently, but his tee shot is above the trees in an instant, then fades artfully from left to right. He's hit the perfect tee shot, at least two hundred and seventy yards down the track.

"Okay," he says to the tee as he withdraws it from the earth, understating his glee. Rhodes is playing to win.

I offer to let Fiona go next, because it seems unfair that she always needs to wait for us. But she mirrors my hand gestures and throws the honour back at me. I don't bother arguing.

I keep my right elbow pressed into my ribs. I push my left shoulder straight down and match it with my left knee. I push against all the resistance from the wildfires inside me, trying to focus my eyesight on a single dimple of the golf ball—the ball marked with a *V. V* for VEIL.

I swing hard. So incredibly hard. The ball-strike vibrates all the way up the shaft of my 4-iron and into my hands, and I know I've hit the hosel of the club.

On impact, a bolt of black travels up my left wrist, into my elbow, then through my shoulder and into the left side of my head. I watch my ball make a leftward beeline toward the circle inside the monastery façade. "Oh, shit," I murmur.

"Uh-oh," Fiona calls out.

As my ball sails through the very centre of the circle, another wave of black pain begins in my left forearm. My left hand seizes up, and I curl into myself. "Oh shit," I exclaim through gritted teeth, and then the black blanket shrouds my eyes again. The turf comes up to meet me as I fall but I don't feel it touch my face.

14

Faith's face is the next thing I see. I reach for her. "No, no, James," I hear a voice call out and a man's hand presses my shoulder. Tears blind me, but I think I make out Rhodes's face coming into view.

A woman's stern voice is what I hear next. "You must stay still, Monsieur Khoury," the voice says, and the blurred vision of Faith's sweet face recedes from view. Things are green here, but not a natural green; it's a light blue-green that looks like mould, moss, or lichen. Or a hospital room.

I hear beeps, loud and frequent. LaBelle's head bobs in and out of view. Tears run down the sides of my face and Rhodes's gloved hand dabs at them with a folded cloth. Rhodes tells LaBelle some numbers, and LaBelle tells

Rhodes to do something I can't quite make out because of the beeps.

As the veil of tears lifts, I see Faith is reaching out for me, holding my right hand as LaBelle works on me to the left, adjusting machines that beep and tubes that drip. I can't feel Faith holding my hand.

I close my eyes, squeezing them shut tightly, as though it could force the golf course to come back and take me away from here.

I open my eyes again.

FISM.

It looks like Faith hasn't slept, and yet she conjures up a tearful smile for me. My mouth is full of something. Suddenly, my throat clenches around a foreign object that's lodged in it and I try to cough. Rhodes presses my forehead back, then injects a needle into my hanging IV bag like he's sliding a tee into the earth. I feel my muscles relax around the tube resting in my trachea, like a flagpole in a cup.

Faith reappears in my view, holding something.

It's a quilt made from all the crests in my Hall of Fame.

Dozens of rayon and terrycloth and cotton and poly-lycra-blend squares arranged by colour into a spectrum of memories that warm me now. Faith dutifully stitched together a totem for the ages, eternally memorializing all my wasted time. Time I could have spent with my family.

She found a way to bring it to me, to this moment.

They say the fall may have caused my brain to swell. They say there's no link between the cancer living in the fluid that keeps my mind safe and the accident. They say they don't know anything for sure, except that I shouldn't expect to escape it.

"This will keep you warm," Faith says, and it's too late for me to reply. I have no time.

Fiona walks into the room, dressed head to toe in white, carrying a clipboard. She asks LaBelle something but her voice is drowned out by a prolonged beep. Fiona puts the clipboard down and walks up to a machine that's behind me. Faith has to move her hand but I shake my head. *Don't let go, Faith. Don't let go of me. Hold on strong. Bring me close.*

Another veil lifts; the veil of memory, and I finally remember what happened:

I'm up on the roof collecting golf balls from the eavestrough, worrying about dirtying my shirt and thinking about Faith, certain she suspects me of cheating.

I see a car driving past the house. I'm not sure, but I think it's Faith. Why isn't she stopping? I'm focused on her, but it's the wrong thing to be focused on, because it means I don't see how close I am to the paper-thin eavestrough. The plastic betrays me as I step forward during my first and only cancer-related seizure, the car upside down and still in my view as I fall to the earth.

I watch her leave. Everything leaves. I fall like a leaf. My foot leaves my shoe stuck in the eavestrough as I fall. I look to the heavens before it goes black.

"Mr. Khoury, can you hear us?" Fiona says loudly.

"Blink once for 'yes,'" Rhodes says, and I do. Faith puts her hands to her face. She wants to look away, I can tell, but she doesn't.

"Please look at me, James," Fiona says, but I don't.

"James we are giving you more fentanyl, which will make you sleep. You've had a fall from a roof."

I blink once. LaBelle murmurs something to Fiona, and I pick up the word "neuro," and Fiona says something containing the word "fragment" but I can't make out the rest. Whatever Fiona says puts a doubtful scowl on LaBelle's face.

"I need you to do something for me, okay?" Fiona projects her voice, like I might be deaf. "Dr. LaBelle is going to poke your toe with her pen. Blink once if you can feel it, twice for 'no,' okay?"

I blink once. Then I wait as long as I can, hoping to feel it, trying to force myself to feel it. *Why can't I feel it?* Tears streaming, I blink a second time.

LaBelle turns to say something to Faith. Maybe all of this is too late. Maybe my sequence is finished.

Where is Payne? I wonder if my son is dead, if I sent him to the other side at the end of our golf game, if I'll ever see him again, and things get murky and blurred, then the lights dim softly. I feel myself falling into a deep void. My feet press into something soft, and then I blink and I can see my shoes partially buried in cream-coloured sand, and I look up and there's a sand cliff, and on the other side I presume is the ninth green, because I have a sand wedge in my hand and I can see the Southwood clubhouse in the distance.

I take the shot and the ball does what I hoped it would do. It flies straight up, gaining enough loft to clear the edge of this monstrous bunker, and disappears over the crest. Without missing a beat, I high-step out of my position and jog up to see beyond the hill, but then I remember myself, my accident, my pain. The hospital room. Where I need to be, under the embrace of my quilt, fighting.

Like a shockwave, remembering myself makes me stumble to the side. Almost on command, the pain comes back.

Which place is real? A trick of the mind? An elaborate fiction?

Rhodes looks back at me from the green. "This is all too real, sorry to say."

Fiona stands up from where she was squatting to survey her shot. "If you lose, you never go back. That's the deal."

Rhodes sizes up his putt. He's above the green and twelve feet from the pin. Fiona has three feet to go. My ball isn't on the green at all.

"We're trying to help you, James. But you need to fight."

Rhodes putts. The ball pounds the back of the cup and settles into it. He pumps a fist.

Fiona picks up her ball. I guess we're done here.

RHODES: 6   FIONA: 2   JAMES: 1

"We need to visit my mom," Faith says. She watches me pull my clubs out from the garage. "You said you'd fix her Wi-Fi."

I have so much to tell her, but I say nothing.

"Are you coming? We have to go."

Payne peers over Faith's shoulder from the kitchen. He keeps his distance.

The rings under Faith's eyes have never been darker. I wonder if we'll ever get ourselves out of this depression. Chi-Chi died, like everyone does. Now we've wasted so much

time not being able to say goodbye, and now my subarach-
noid space is contaminated, and now we must say goodbye
to each other.

I say nothing. I get my clubs and head for the backyard to
practice my short game.

A few minutes later, I am swinging my clubs and they
leave, without saying goodbye.

15

THE BACK NINE

I don't bother retrieving my ball. I don't utter a word as we make our way to the tenth, past the clubhouse and through an empty parking lot. The summer sun hasn't relinquished its hold on this place, and its warmth eases some of the tension in my muscles.

I fell from the roof of the garage after my family drove away. After I drove them away. I think about all the time I spent in the backyard and on golf courses, all by myself, for the past thirty years. I think about my lost playing partners: Chi-Chi. Faith. My son. My brother.

We've been mired since Chi-Chi died. But it wasn't Chi-Chi's fault. It was mine. It was all the things I didn't do that led us to that moment where they drove away and weren't there to see me fall. We had fallen already.

Now here I am, so arrogant that I thought I had some special role to play in the afterlife. Like I was an angel of some kind. But I'm only a duffer. With the ball as a physical manifestation of my intention, I hack and slice and hook, then call it a stroke of brilliance and a gentle fade. A power draw. I love playing but I've played it wrong from the beginning. My intention brought me off-course every single time.

Finally, after all that's happened to me and within me, I understand clearly and completely that I am playing for survival, trapped inside the neural links. Playing a mental game. This is all playing out in the exclusive golf and country club of my subconscious. I am trying to defeat my doctors and nurse so I can come back to life.

The stakes: a mulligan.

How I would love a mulligan for all of it.

I would do things so differently if I could try again. I would pour all of myself into Faith. I would hold her until she feels strong enough to decimate me with a single quip, like in the before times. I would beg her to be my playmate, and we would be a twosome for all the time we had left. I would never keep score. I would tell her we are here, together, for a short time longer, in the sequence of one step after the next, and I don't want to go it alone ever again.

Nothing would ever come between us. Nothing and no one.

In the wind and the grass of this golf course, something else is here, making up the rules and keeping us honest. Something further in, or further up that we can't see pulls the strings and keeps us on the fairway. I know it's inside me. And I know it's watching. Judging.

I do the math as we reach the tenth tees: I need at least eight of nine, and for Fiona to win the one I can't. I'm going to need some help from my doctor to make this miracle happen. Otherwise, Rhodes gets to be the angel of mercy he's looking to be. It's going to be nearly impossible to keep him off the board for the entirety of the back nine when he's just taken down two-thirds of the front.

Five tee boxes run at an angle from the left to right, like a hand of playing cards. The par-4 is long and doglegs left. Of course, it wouldn't be complete without a vortex of a bunker placed right where the golfer would want to aim, where a typical drive would land if you make any error in execution. Perhaps Thomas McBroom is the devil, here where I am.

With his five-skin monster victory, Rhodes has the honour. He smashes a towering drive that rises so quickly I lose it in the blue of the sky. I shield my eyes from the glare of the sun and watch the ground for bounces.

"I lost that one," I tell him.

"There," Fiona points at his ball, presently rolling along the contour of the fairway, three hundred yards away from us.

I can't muster any kind of compliment for him. Watching the perfection of that drive twists a knife into my back. I expel some steamy breath through my nose and slide my tee into the earth. I'm not hitting my shot three hundred yards, no matter what I do.

Like the Tin Man, I have to work against rusted joints to straighten up and tilt my right side down ever so slightly. I look at the ball to ensure it's aligned to the left, toward the inside of my left foot. I remember to keep my grip loose, my wrists and forearms ready to apply the final blow, like a hammer hitting a nail, or a boxer landing an uppercut.

"Relax and do what you can," Rhodes says to me softly.

I drop my club to the ground and spin on a heel. "No advice," I bark at him.

He sticks his hands up in self-defence. "Jeez, sorry."

"You're not my coach and you're not my guardian angel, all right?"

"Easy, James."

"You're not my friend." It occurs to me that I had fancifully thought of him as all three.

"I was trying to help."

"Play the game, you guys," Fiona says as she pulls her bag to the green tees. "Don't delay the inevitable any longer that we have to."

Sound medical advice.

"You heard her," Rhodes says.

I drop my left shoulder down and reach as far back as I can. I start the forward motion with the tiniest of club head drops, then use my lower body to propel the big muscles in my back and shoulders. Arms and club uncoil around my head like spring-loaded clockwork. I make good contact, and it's plain for everyone to hear.

On a golf course, the most satisfying sound is the sound of the ball striking the bottom of the cup. Second to that has to be the sound of a driver struck in the centre of the club face. That *whoosh* just prior to the crackling *ping* of echoing metal composites and plastic polymers that is the sum total of your most violent, controlled outburst on the course. That's the sound I generate with this drive. It is perfect.

I'd throw eighteen consecutive perfect sounds away to hear Faith's whisper in my ear once more.

I don't need to see the ball in flight. I look down at the tee and withdraw its fragments from the ground, some of them embedded in the turf like rib fragments in lungs, or skull fragments in brain.

"Great shot," Rhodes says. "Cleared the bunker and found some safety." Fiona flashes a thumbs up from fifty yards ahead. They can be as nice as they want. I am winning this.

Fiona's drive also finds safe purchase, off to the right but parallel to the fairway bunker. Our second shots don't distinguish us much from one another; my three-wood makes as good a *ping* as I've ever been able to generate with it, and the resulting shot travels low and nearly straight, but short. I roll it up the checkerboard approach to the green and it stops midway up the slope. Fiona's shot leaves her a solid fifty yards from the elevated green. Rhodes skies a 9-iron, and a summer breeze pulls it off course. It lands on the fringe of the green, but its momentum bounces it off the dance floor and down the slope, out of sight.

Par looks like it may be enough to win this hole, but I'm thinking birdie. Fiona uses an 8-iron to chip her way up the hill and onto the green. She's nowhere close to the pin. I try to visualize holing out from here; flopping one that spins back and into the cup. I know it's unrealistic for a person with my skills, but this isn't reality. This is dreamland. Maybe the laws of physics and probability don't apply. Maybe I can believe. Maybe I can will myself to victory.

Ball back in the stance, open club face, try to lift the follow-through up high to generate backspin… it doesn't work. I hit it fat and make a divot the size of a toupée. My ball doesn't get high enough. I make it to the green, but the spin is all wrong. I'm ten feet from the hole. It gives Rhodes a chance to win with this chip shot, but he doesn't have the touch and sculls it, leaving him four feet away with a makeable par putt.

I need to make this putt to prevent Rhodes from winning, and to give myself that chance. I have to keep believing. I survey the break, address the ball, and run through my checklist. I try to focus on what my feet sense beneath them. *Relax the arms, use the big muscles, and line up the centre line on the putter's head with the heart of the ball.* I mimic a pendulum as much as I can and send the ball on its way.

Boom.

The putt drops and I pump my fist. I look to the sky but it's less of a "thank you" and more of a "fuck you," and whoever pulls the strings around here doesn't appreciate my petulance. Rhodes sinks his four-foot par putt with ease. The skin carries over.

I say nothing to the others. As soon as I hear the grating sound of Rhodes's ball echoing in the cup, I march ahead to try and beat them again.

I'll win the two skins up for grabs at the eleventh, then. No problem.

Water awaits the golfer who under-hits the par-3 eleventh. The green starts at two hundred yards and only has about ten feet of leeway around its edge before it plunges you into the drink. The front half of the green is visible from the tees, sloping hard. Just past the crest of the slope, I can see the tip of the white flag.

Rhodes arrives and I gesture to him to have the honour. Rhodes pulls out a 5-iron and aims at the water. He's going to try a fade, so the ball will roll less. It works. The shot ambles from left to right gracefully, soars above the pond, and falls lazily onto the green. But once the momentum is drained from his shot, it rolls down the slope with increasing speed, visible to all three of us. The front edge of the green collects it at the bottom, probably twenty paces from the hole and ten feet beneath it. It's a gimmicky mini-golf putt for birdie.

I barely give Rhodes time to make way for me. I don't bother with a tee; the lie is perfect enough. I hold my three-wood, my two-hundred-yard club. With determination, I set up to the right of the target, but not too far right, ball in the middle of the stance, down and back, one, two, follow through, from the inside out: *PING.*

The draw is low and doesn't move to the left the way I expected it to. It arrives almost exactly where Rhodes's ball came to rest, but the subsequent roll shoots it up the slope so hard that it becomes airborne. I have no idea where it goes after that.

This is a shot that amicable golfers, enjoying a round of communion with nature, would need to discuss. That's the whole point of being out here, isn't it? To share with others how your intentions translate to reality in the context of the physical world? But I say nothing. This isn't golf. This is a battle.

Fiona lays up. She hits a 9-iron a hundred yards, clean

and easy, and lands it at the end of the wide part of the fairway, past the hazard.

Laying up on a par-3 isn't going to win you the skins. FISM, Fiona.

On her second shot, she lobs it straight up and the ball goes straight down, along the same line as the flag. Rhodes tells her it's a good one. She salutes with her fingers to thank him.

Finally, we get to the green and I run up the hill to assess my situation. I push the pain out of my mind, but gravity makes sure I remember my age and failing abilities. I'm winded after the sprint up the steep grade. But the situation is excellent: the cup sits at the bottom of a small basin, and my ball has come to rest at the top of that basin, about four feet away from the cup. I'll need to mark it because Fiona's shot is on exactly the same line, some eight feet from the hole. Rhodes and I each have birdie putts, but Rhodes will need a miracle.

He doesn't get one. Before I can even put the dime down to mark my putt, Rhodes plays a wedge shot to flop his way to the cup. His shot goes way left and Fiona has to dodge it as she sizes up her putt. He's on the green, thirty feet away. We can only see the top of his head as he concedes.

Fiona takes an extremely gentle stroke that comes off the putter lightly, and the ball goes from zero to sixty down the run of the basin. The line is off by a fraction and the speed is unforgiving; her ball circles the lip and zips three feet past.

I know what to do. The weight. The line. Big muscles. No pressure. Like ice in a glass.

RHODES: 6   JAMES: 3   FIONA: 2

I stare Rhodes down. Nothing is going to stop me. I feel something I've never felt before on a golf course: dominance.

If the surface of the moon was green, it would look a lot like the twelfth hole. Five bunkers rise out of the layout like volcanic craters, including one that splits the fairway in two. It's less than three hundred and fifty yards from the blue tees to the flagstick, which is short for a par-4, but the feature sand trap is exactly two hundred and fifty yards away, and almost no one can carry their driver that far in the air. But a lot of people can make their shot roll that far. It's a true sand trap; devious and brilliant. I lay up.

I have the honour, so Fiona and Rhodes get to see my strategy, which is fine with me. I want Rhodes to think he should go for it. I want to force him into mistakes and shake his confidence. I want to show him my mettle. I want to show him how my privileges were earned, and how the course has toughened me, like physical therapy, and now I am strong enough to win my privileges back.

I hit the mound leading up to the sand trap and that rolls my ball leftward. It comes to a stop safely on the narrow strip of intermediate cut between fairway and fescue. I'm safe and I'm a hundred and twenty yards away. Not even the numbness in my shoulder, shooting down to the tip of my left pinky finger, can distract me from feeling good about that one.

Rhodes nods to himself and pulls out his driver. He widens his stance, like he wants to demolish the golf ball.

His warm-up swings don't flow like they did before. With a clenched jaw that makes his temples tumescent, he annihilates his tee with a stroke that nearly flips the club on the follow-through. The contact sounds like a gunshot. Rhodes is forced to take a step forward, his momentum is so great. The ball flies exactly two hundred and fifty yards, right into the craterous centre sand trap. I look down to suppress a grin.

"Well, that wasn't very bright," Fiona says him, and I can't help but chuckle.

Rhodes looks down at the face of his driver like he's going to ask it why it did that.

He makes his way over to his FISM and chops at his bunker shot, wipes it way right with an uncharacteristic lack of grace. He mutters something to himself that's muffled by the flying sand, and gazes at the fescue about sixty yards ahead. A true duff. Rhodes pollutes the air with his vitriol as he walks over to where his shot landed.

From where I am with my second shot, I can see an embankment on the back of this green that will let me play with my roll and stay safe. Fiona, who cleared the fairway bunker easily from the ladies' tees, uses the same strategy from one hundred and forty yards away, hitting a stock 7-iron shot that hits the heart of the green and rolls upward toward the back, leaving her with a makeable birdie putt. Not a certainty, but makeable.

I get to use a 9-iron, which is the club I used to teach Payne how to play when he was a small boy. I remember having him open his palms and then bring his hands together at his belly button like a classical singer, then gently laying the grip of the 9-iron into his palms. I wrapped my fingers around his and closed each one, gently and lovingly. "Hold on, but not too tight," I said to him, and he nodded as he looked up at me with eyes that still saw me as something more than human. A god. A father.

I got frustrated with him because he got frustrated with his mistakes. He didn't love golf the way I did, because of me. A child doesn't need to pretend they have control of something, and I did.

The 9-iron shot gets closer to the heavens than I anticipated and I nearly lose sight of the ball before it comes down on the green, a body-length away from pay dirt, and bounces exactly once before a sudden stop. Perfect.

Rhodes appears with no ball and a red face. "Go," he grunts to Fiona. Fiona goes. She's fifteen feet for birdie. Her line is perfect, but the weight isn't right and her ball breaks too much to the left, leaving her a foot away from par.

I sink the putt and win again. I hide my glee from the other two, but as I look away, I furtively pump my fist. *I'm coming, everybody. I'm coming.*

RHODES: 6   JAMES: 4   FIONA: 2

"You're playing real good," Fiona says to me as we walk together.

"I know you're my doctor," I tell her. "I'm in my head right now. I know that, you know. This isn't real."

From the look on her face, I think Fiona doesn't agree. "Real isn't what you think it is," she says. "Reality's what your mind makes for you to deal with things. But real is more than that."

"Well, Doc, I've got my mind made up. I'm not leaving them."

"Everybody leaves, Mr. Khoury," Fiona says, and that shuts me right up.

I look left from the blue tees and find the fattest part of the fairway, left of the one-fifty marker. It's an easy 6-iron across the water with plenty of wiggle room for bad contact, but I hit it fine. I'm past the danger and looking at another 6-iron to get to the green.

Rhodes silently pulls out his driver and blasts the tee shot without even looking. It's got plenty of distance to clear the drink, but it's right. Way right. He's either in the fescue or the water, depending on the unseen bounce. If it's safe, he's a hundred yards away. We all look at each other. Nobody saw how it finished.

Fiona's tee box is down a narrow path of manicured grass and her vantage point looks completely different than from the blue tees. She gets a straight-ahead look at the flagstick and only needs to loft her ball maybe a hundred and fifty yards to be safe. She pulls out the driver. Power draw. It tickles the left bank of the fairway but appears to stay on the short stuff, sixty yards ahead of me. She's in great shape.

Now it should be Faith's turn. We could be couples, golfing as a foursome, if she was here. It would feel right. There's a rhythm to golf, and with LaBelle quitting the game—to see other patients, perhaps?—the rhythm seems off. It's because there's something missing. Faith is missing.

I dig out my 4-iron, calculate the distance, and wipe some sweat from my forehead. *Will to win,* I tell myself. *I'm in control here.* The banked front bunker and glaring sun combine to make me lose track of my shot as it lands on the green. Fiona congratulates me, Rhodes does not, and we continue onward.

One ball is about eight feet away from the flagstick and the other about twenty.

"Whose is whose?" I ask Fiona. She shrugs.

Rhodes gets some luck, if luck exists here. He finds his ball beneath a few tufts of the tall yellow grass, but not mangled up in it. He can muscle through the fescue, and he does, landing on the front of the green. The roll gets him three feet from the cup. My stomach starts to twist up.

We inspect the golf balls and I see the three-dot marking on the twenty-footer. My stomach twists tighter. Fiona and Rhodes both mark as I prepare.

I can sense the left-to-right break with my toes. I try to go through my checklist, but Faith needs to be here. All I can see is every wrinkle of her time-worn face, and eyes that have lived a life with me, and the vestiges of her youth that have become a deeper, more beautiful image of love.

I push her out of my mind and putt, but the result is a huge error—a chicken-shit putt. I don't even propel the ball far enough to pass Rhodes's marker, six feet away. Calamity. I start calculating: five holes left, I'm down two to Rhodes ... I need to cheer for Fiona here.

Thankfully, Fiona holds up her end of the bargain, draining a beauty that rides the break with authority. Rhodes can carry it over, but the putt rings around the lip and stays out. He closes his eyes, like he was expecting it.

RHODES: 6   JAMES: 4   FIONA: 3

The par-5 fourteenth is laid out like a wrinkled blanket that zigzags left and then right. It's not even a close one. Fiona wins. I'm in trouble.

Rhodes's shots are consistently off and his rage begins to boil, to the point where he may as well be playing alone.

Together, yet alone. I know that feeling. I'm no stranger to anger. I've tossed clubs, hit my bag with them, yelled at them, grounded them for a week, sent them to club jail with the other failed clubs in the Golf Zone of my garage. I've felt like a golf club has betrayed me. When you're fiery with emotion, you don't even realize what you're saying. Something inside you suggests that you can make this inanimate object into a companion with a life of its own, one that has the ability to disobey what you're commanding it to do, or stab you in the back when you need it the most.

So when Rhodes roars "COME ON!" at his entire bag, it's pathetic more than anything. Even though I need to beat him, I've been there. I'm simply ahead of him in the sequence.

Meanwhile, I'm short and low with all five of my approach shots, and it takes me all five to figure out that my hands are arriving ahead of the club face.

Fiona's shots are unspectacular but right where she needs them to be. She's focused on the right thing.

RHODES: 6   FIONA: 4   JAMES: 4

Disaster strikes on the fifteenth. I overcompensate and keep my hands too far back on the driver. The tee shot goes farther upward than it does outward. I don't even get the shot to the fairway. It's embarrassing.

Rhodes finally connects with a proper tee shot, which for him is nearly three hundred yards in length and right down the middle of the fairway. He slides his driver back into the bag like he's sheathing Excalibur.

Fiona can't compete with that, and neither can I. Only Rhodes's terrible putting can hold him back, and I swear he closes his eyes as he strokes a ten-foot putt for birdie. He takes the skin, and with three holes left, I'm three skins back.

We trudge into the river valley that leads us back to the monastery and clubhouse. I have to take all three skins, just for a tie. It's beginning to feel impossible.

"Nothing's impossible, Mr. Khoury," Fiona says. She rests a hand on my shoulder. "It's all inside you."

I know it's all inside me. That doesn't seem to change the rules here.

"What kind of hokum is that, Fiona? I thought you were a doctor."

"I am a doctor, and that's why I don't like calling it your heart. Because, anatomically, it isn't your heart. All the same, you're focused on the wrong thing."

"What the hell am I supposed to focus on, Fiona? My hands? The ball? The target?"

"Love," she says. "Focus on love when you golf, Mr. Khoury."

RHODES: 7   FIONA: 4   JAMES: 4

Three holes left to find a way back to my life and the ones I love.

"What happens if we tie?" I ask no one in particular.

No one answers.

The La Salle River is directly to our right, and for the first time, we enter the river grove. Elm and oak trees abound, almost as though this final set of holes is in another world. The sun is obstructed here, cooling the air and casting everything in shadow. The earth is softer. I remember the tire fire that was my previous round at Southwood: how I hacked my 7-iron all the way down the final three holes in an act of utter, resentful resignation. There were aphids everywhere, and mosquitoes in the shadows, and Asian lady beetles that would bite your legs. There was the occasional locust. But now, the only life here is the greenery and the three of us, and the breath of the creator, Thomas McBroom, inhabiting all of it.

The hole breaks hard to the left, extremely hard, and you can't see the green from the tees at all. The slope is strange along the riverbank: it looks as though it slopes from right to left, but the ball goes left to right as it rolls along the fairway. All three of us make our tee shots, Fiona and I with our less-than-long drivers and Rhodes with a three-wood. The fairway is forgiving enough to let each of us stay aboard. *Why isn't life forgiving?* I wonder. The answer comes right away: if life was easy, if you couldn't make mistakes and lose what you've got, those things wouldn't be special. They wouldn't be rare. Exactly like a golf course. The easy ones don't get remembered.

The green is parked on a hump that drains any shot that rolls, spilling it off to the sides. And if it's short, you will either land at the bottom of a deep ravine or into one of two hand-shaped bunkers that appear to be telling you to stop, whoa, turn back now. Like God has crafted this hole with his bare hands. Or the Devil.

Panicked, my mind races to calculate the distance and club, the breadth and length of the hazards, to try and shape a shot that will generate less spin. How much loft can I achieve and still hit it one hundred and seventy yards?

I decide to club up, to a 5-iron, and then try to create a fade with hands slightly behind the ball on impact, club face marginally open, swing plane a fraction to the inside of the ball, because infinitesimally small changes and adjustments are what make a good golf shot, just like life. You make small adjustments.

It doesn't work. My shot spills off to the right. I throw my hands up and then grip my head, trying to still the reverberating waves of pain that worsen as my heart rate goes up.

Fiona plays it safe with a 9-iron, which gets her into the ravine at least ten yards beneath the green. An 8-iron gets Rhodes the one hundred and sixty yards he needs. His ball bites into the green and spins backward a foot. A gorgeous shot. "Wow," Fiona says in admiration.

Fiona manages to flop a lovely wedge shot straight up to gain the elevation she needs, but it's not quite straight enough. I rush to survey my ball and my chances to salvage this hole. The game could be lost—everything could be lost—if I flub this.

I'm off the green, but not by much. I can chip it, get

close, and then hope Rhodes's putting is as poor as it's been for most of this round.

Fight, James. Fight for your family. It comes to me like a disembodied voice.

I start to go through my checklist and analysis of the green, and then I realize what I need to do.

For lack of a better word, and in the least medical sense possible, I need to play with my heart. The biggest muscle. With love. With my insides out.

I let them out.

I've never golfed with tears streaming down my face before, or with arms going numb. I've golfed while nauseated, but it had never before been triggered by how much I feel like I've failed my wife and son. I've never played while seeing myself from a thousand miles above, from behind the sky, observing how insignificant I am as I attempt to conquer the infinite for one microscopic and futile moment, like dividing one by infinity. I've never played like a beggar asking for a place to sleep. I've never thought about what I would give for one more look into the sparkling eyes of my one true love, and the life we created together. I'll never have a chance to see them again if I don't take a shot.

I golf from the inside, from my heart, and I let it guide my intention, and the ball behaves, bound by the inertia of my desperation, the momentum of my need to get back to them, the gravity of my love. The ball obeys. I beat nature.

With a bounce, a roll, and a clink, I hole out the chip shot.

I look to the sky. "Thank God."

"There's no God up there," Rhodes says.

244

"Whatever. Just putt." I wipe my eyes.

"You think God's up there?"

"No, Rhodes. Play. Please."

"He's around. Just not up there."

Rhodes pushes the putt right. I win the skin.

RHODES: 7   JAMES: 5   FIONA: 4

Seventeenth hole. Par-3.

It's wide open, one hundred and sixty yards to the flag-stick, located at the back of the green. I can roll right up to it.

I don't think about my shot. Instead, I remember the people I've met as I've been golfing in ... wherever this is. My mind, I guess? I didn't even get to golf a round with Lane before he was gone. I let myself be angry with God, but then I remember that I probably *am* God here. It was still me.

Drawing from right to left, my ball lands mid-green, makes a single bounce, and rolls left to right, closer and closer to the hole, and suddenly I am barking, "Go! Go!" hoping I might make my first hole in one.

The ball comes to rest a foot left of the cup. There's no way I'm not finishing this hole in two.

Fiona and Rhodes each make the green, but they're nowhere near as close as I am. We make our way to the putting surface, silently. I can barely walk now. The pain is in every nerve fibre, making me feel like I'm a tin man who's run out of oil. I strain to lift my foot from the ground with every step. My head is throbbing, and my back, my ribs ... I've had a fall. What am I doing golfing when I've had a fall?

No. I have to win. As we reach the green, I reach for my ball marker: Chi-Chi's dime. It's the only golf-related keepsake I have from him. I remember in those first weeks after he died, when reality was too painful to face head-on, Faith's mom Dorothy would find dimes everywhere, and she swore it was silly but admitted to thinking, "Maybe that's Chi-Chi putting a marker down for me, like a secret message." But I knew better. I knew it wasn't a secret message. It wasn't a secret at all. He was marking his putt so people could keep playing through.

"Tap it in," Rhodes says, and so I pocket the dime. I don't need long to be sure of what I'm doing. It's straight in, and that sound eases me enough to almost take a full breath.

Rhodes smacks his putt with almost no preparation, and as it hurtles toward the cup, he starts to put body English on it, trying to gesture it into the hole.

It goes in. The skin carries over to the eighteenth.

"Well, I guess this is it," I say to my opponents. "Thanks for taking care of me. Thanks for giving me a chance."

"Keep on fighting," Fiona says. "We can tell you're a fighter."

"I bet you say that to all the golfers," I tell her.

16

LAST CHANCE

We're at the longest hole on the course, the par-5 eighteenth. From our elevated tee box some five hundred and fifteen yards away, we can see the sprawling entirety of it; a hard dogleg right, with the river cutting in. The slope sweeps powerfully toward the water, and the mischievous golf deity McBroom has placed his bunkers in exactly the five possible spots one might need to reach the green with efficiency. From this elevation, Rhodes and I can see the monastery ruins peeking out beyond the clubhouse roof.

I've been a monk.

I took a vow of golfing, to try and constantly improve on something that proves absolutely nothing. And at what expense? I golfed to connect, and yet golfing disconnected me from the people I love the most. But golfing is who I am, even if I did it alone, or with strangers, or with ghosts.

"Why?" Rhodes asks me. "Why do you need to get better? Why not play for the sake of playing?"

As I stare out at the monastery, the answer finds me. "I need to get better because I need to express myself in this world better. I want the shot to reflect my intent."

Fiona looks back at us like she knows we're talking big picture.

"You," Rhodes takes a practice swing like punctuation, "aren't being the ball."

I place my tee in the grass for a final time. "I don't even know what the hell that means, Rhodes."

"When all the physical forces are too much for you … when they've had their way with you … you need to come to rest. You're trying to keep rolling, man, but every ball loses the fight to keep going. You'll come to rest too, James. It's okay."

"No way in hell." I let my driver rip, inviting the pain to have its way with me. My knees buckle as the ball flies left, a beautiful ascent like an aircraft rising above Kitty Hawk, proving something to reality itself. We are human beings. We never rest.

The ball heads straight for a left-side bunker, but it hits the ryegrass of the fairway and rides the slope to the right. That's my longest drive, ever. I think it might be three hundred yards, when you factor in the roll. I'm only getting stronger. I'm not golfing with my body anymore.

"Nice shot," Rhodes says, and then casually rips the exact same shot so similar that his ball comes to rest two feet behind mine.

Fiona has a fifty-yard head start on us, which is nothing on this hole. She manages to get ahead of us, but anywhere you go on this fairway, you end up at the bottom of a bowl. She's only one bowl ahead. A good shot will get any of us onto the green in two, putting for eagle.

"The doctor wants me to keep fighting. You just want to win," I tell Rhodes.

"You know what the difference is between a doctor and a nurse?" he asks.

I shrug.

"A doctor fixes you. A nurse takes care of you."

I use the biggest muscle of all, bigger than my shoulders and back and hamstrings put together. I let my heart pour out, into my hands, into the shaft of the club as it draws back. I release all the fear I ever held onto until my face curdles into a weep. If I don't get home, I don't get to prove that I'm worth loving. I don't get to know whether Payne is alive or dead. I don't get to help Faith with the fragments of whatever life is left for her to try and piece together. But mostly the fear is that I'm not enough. Not enough to be a man in the world, to provide and support and be worthy of love. That's why I wanted to be better at this game. I'm afraid of not getting better, because what I am isn't good enough.

The club flies out of my hands on the follow-through and Rhodes has to limbo backward as it helicopters past him. "Sorry! Sorry!" I say to him and I go and fetch the club.

"Um?" Rhodes grabs me by the shoulder and spins me holeward. He points at the green.

My ball is on there.

It looks like maybe three feet for eagle.

Ahead of us, Fiona flashes me a thumbs up.

"I'm not sure I should even take this shot," Rhodes says. "But I will. Because if I win, then you'll stop fighting, and that's what's best, James. I promise you. Sometimes struggling isn't what's best."

"I'll never stop fighting, Rhodes. I'm leaving here."

Rhodes addresses his ball with a muscular waggle of the club.

"I admire your fortitude, man," he tells me. "But you made a deal. If you lose, you stop resisting."

I have learned the ultimate lesson: go through the sequence using your heart, not your head. I finally learned that you can't think your way through all of it. When it comes down to the final, most critical moment, you need to let your soul do the muscle work.

Rhodes lets his muscles do the muscle work. He crushes the ball, dominates it, and I wonder if it might not get all the way to the monastery before gravity gets hold of it. It bounces on the asphalt cart path that runs behind the green, which makes it shoot straight up and into the forest. It's a goner.

Fiona takes her time with her set-up, long enough for me and Rhodes to join her at the edge of the depression she's in. "You're doing what you can," Fiona says to me as she sits down in her stance. "We see it. You've done well."

I know she's not talking about golf. I don't respond.

Her shot leaves her a twenty-yard chip shot to get there, and she'd have to hole out to make three. I need a three-foot putt.

As we make our final walk down the fairway, as one does with every final walk, I reflect on the round and pull myself out of the moment. Gratitude rises up inside me. I've changed. In just eighteen holes, I've let go of so much.

"Thank you," I tell them. "For the game. I've learned a lot, and that's why I'm out here."

"Says more about you than you want it to, right?" Fiona says, and I couldn't agree with her more.

The sun finds a clear path to us as the trees recede and we reach Fiona's ball, nestled in some short grass, glimmering in the light twenty yards away and well below the green.

"This is it," Rhodes says. "Fiona needs to hole this out, or you get to make a putt for the skin."

There's a sound and Rhodes stiffens up. It's LaBelle coming up the course in the red marshal's cart, and she parks it beside Fiona.

"We need a decision on what's next here," Fiona says to her.

"If the results are in Monsieur Khoury's favour, then we'll continue this course, I think," LaBelle says. Her face is cast in shadow, beneath the canopy of the cart. I'm not sure if she's referring to another hole on the golf course, or a course of treatment, and I'm blurring the two places again.

"Okay," Fiona says, and it occurs to me that LaBelle must be the attending physician, or whatever they call the boss of the intensive care unit, and Fiona is an ICU resident in charge of taking care of me on the ward.

I try to prepare myself for my putt. Fiona readies herself, but not for too long. She looks up at me, mid-process, and her shoulders relax. She interrupts herself to tell me, "You're focused on the right things, right now, James. Keep at it."

Her ball stops midway up the hill, and she offers me a warm look. She doesn't want to just fix me. She cares. She sees I'm trying to cooperate.

I'm coming home. I know I'm coming home; I know it in my broken bones, and I'm going to heal up and defeat death to get back to the love of my family, and the ball travels like a bubble in an IV tube along the bentgrass and injects itself into the cup.

JAMES: 7   RHODES: 7   FIONA: 4

17

NINETEENTH HOLE

The echo of my skin-winning shot has barely filled the air when the black flash returns and we stand at the blue tees of the iconic ninth, with its view of the monastery to the left and clubhouse behind the green.

Fiona and LaBelle are gone. It's me and Rhodes. Rhodes polishes the face of his driver with a white towel. Suddenly, he takes a massive breath in through his nose.

"God, that smell," he says. "I love that. Nothing like all that nature waking you up with a single smell."

I try to breathe in through my nose, but I can't. I nod, but I can't smell anything.

"Better than a cup of coffee," Rhodes says.

I swing my club three times, and a fourth, trying not to remember how this hole went the first time around.

"So here we are, James. Sudden death. Just the two of us. Excited?"

"I think I'm more tired than anything. But I'm still going to beat your ass."

"Get us started," Rhodes says, and backs away so I can tee off. I avoid looking at that damn monastery window, the circle with nothing but the heavens showing through it. I try to square up my shoulders and then tilt them a bit to start my drive.

Rhodes talks behind me. "You know why we look to the sky for God? Because our eyes can't look inward."

Whatever's inside me shoots a horrid blast of pain into my ribs as I come around on my shot. I drop my club. I can't help but look to the heavens, through the circular frame of the empty monastery window, and as soon as the ball flies into the frame all over again, I am gone.

Beeps and frantic motion all around me. Blurs of electric blue and ice green. I don't see Faith's face, only her ponytail as she leaves the room. Talking, so much talking … the pain crushes me, sits on me like a collapsed building, paralyzing me. LaBelle's face is too close to mine, and she turns back to bark something at Rhodes. I open my eyes wider to see Fiona behind them, arms folded, looking angry. She holds a clipboard, looks at the numbers on it, then shakes her head and tosses the clipboard in frustration. Then there's a solid line of sound, a single tone, like a pitch pipe that prepares the choir to sing its hallelujahs, a uniting tone that soothes me.

The skin doesn't carry over to some other place. I am here. I am dying. I am coming to rest.

The electric blue and ice green become muted and

mottled. They darken. We all darken and weaken. We all leave.

Rhodes brings his lips to my ear. "I'll take care of you now."

Things go black, for a time.

And then the veil lifts. I am lucid but unable to control myself. The medical staff stand back, the same distance one would give a golfer whose turn it is to impart their intentions on an insignificant little ball, trying to send it to its final resting place.

Faith sits in the chair across from me, wiping her nose with a tissue. I'm all bundled up in my quilt like a swaddled baby. The tubes dangle beside me. Disconnected.

Above us is a television, absent-mindedly left on, perhaps while I was comatose and stable. Scott Branch wears a sheriff's badge on the screen.

And then, walking into the doorway, I see my son. Payne. Alive. My body tenses up. I want to swallow and jump up and scream and hold him, but first I have to swallow, and I can't do that.

Tears stream down Payne's face. He sits down beside me and I do everything I can to send him a signal, to tell him I love him, that I wanted to be better, that he doesn't deserve this. Payne reaches for my hand and I can feel his touch, which makes me happy. I think I have tears running down my face. I am playing this with my heart.

Payne places something in my palm and closes my fingers around it. He takes both of his hands and raises my forearm, pressing my fist against his cheek. *Don't cry, my boy. I'll always be here. Don't cry so much. Grandpa says to listen to your folks, eat your cereal, get to bed before midnight.*

I look behind my hand pressed against his cheek. There's no tattoo on Payne's neck.

Whatever Payne has placed in my hand feels rough and hard. Dimpled. I open up my fingers and see what he's given me, and it makes both Payne and Faith perk up with wonderment, like I'm not supposed to do that. I see what's in my hand: a golf ball.

A golf ball with a heart drawn on it, in pink permanent marker.

It rolls out of my hand and bounces with a loud crack on the floor, and LaBelle leaps into the room to tell my family it was probably an automatic reflex response, and don't be too hopeful—all this is simply a mechanical, physical process, and we don't know what's going on inside of James, but it is time to say our goodbyes. Faith hasn't let go of my other hand. I can feel her holding on. I can feel the energy exchange between us like telegraph wires.

I'm coming to a rest. I've left divots. I've played the course. And now the sun sets, as it does on every one of us, on every round, no matter the player. I'm not afraid anymore. No one gets what they want. Everyone leaves.

18

VICTORIA BEACH

Pale, golden sunlight diffuses through a crystal-blue sky, unlike any other place I've ever been, and I know by looking skyward that I'm at Victoria Beach again. Heaven.

This time, there's no secret message in the metal contraption at the first tees. There's one ball, and it isn't mine. It is adorned with a pink heart.

"Looks like we're up," a voice says from behind me, and it makes the hairs on my neck stand on end. I spin around and there's a sparkle in Faith's pale blue eyes. She's dressed in her best golf gear and smiles a smile that could sink a thousand putts. It makes me feel like I'm the centre of her universe.

I wrap my arms around her. There's no pain anymore,

not a lick of it. Only the pleasure of finally being with her, even if it isn't in the world we made for ourselves. I'll take this as a consolation.

"I'm so happy to see you," I bawl into her ear. "So glad to golf with you again."

As I sniffle, I breathe in the lake air and it opens me up. I look up to the heavens, to the sky the same blue as my true love's eyes, and I ready myself for the round.

Faith takes my hand and pulls me to the tee box.

There was a time when I would wish I could spend eternity on this course with this woman. But golf isn't heaven. It's something much, much better. It's life.

It doesn't matter how good the tee shots are, or where the balls end up. I have so much I want to say to her, but the words won't come. Instead, I say, "Nice shot," even if it might not be.

As we walk through the trees between the second and third, I finally tell her, "Golf was too much and I wasn't enough, Faith. But wherever I golfed, there I was. It was still me. Fuck."

She stops, and turns back to face me. "God, is that what you think? You are my everything, James. All of it. It's a life together. Let's live it."

We get to the tee box. I grab a club with a number on it, take a whack at the ball. I watch it curve up and over the tall elm on the left, then strike the fringe of the hilly green and roll right into the cup. An ace.

"What do you want to do now?" I ask her.

"Let's go for a walk on the beach."

We deposit our clubs at the cottage. Payne's there, reading *How To Win Friends and Influence People*, a dusty copy he found while exploring the antique shelves of this place. He's happy to join us.

We saunter down King Edward Avenue, alone together, us in nature, quiet with our thoughts.

"Even the bad times are not so bad, I think," I tell Faith as we reach the steps to the beach.

She nods in agreement through her tears. "Bad times are better than no times." We smile for each other.

"You should take your mom and go to that bar in Scotland," I say to her. "You go get your dad's golf ball, and then you have a drink for both of us."

She nods again.

I send all of my intention through my hand into hers, far, far from Victoria Beach Golf Course.

She nods, and our embrace loosens. Erodes.

When it's gone, you lose everything. When the zeitgeist doesn't need you anymore, all the issues become meaningless and you go beyond the sequence. You lose your identity. You lose all privilege. All the markings you've left and the achievements you made, everything leaves, lost to history. All you have left is the giddy shriek of laughter from the one you love; a dance through the sand, your footsteps cast in the divine providence of a sunset; moments frozen in time, like the frozen end of a perfect follow-through.

I watch the sunset with my camera in my hand, snapping photos of Faith and Payne while they walk through the sand, twisting their feet with each step like a summer dance that propels them through paradise; they are bathed in light from the crimson sunset, which paints shadows into each sandy footstep they leave behind. Faith's red hoodie matches Payne's bathing suit. I kneel in genuflection, taking picture after picture, moved to the verge of tears by the beauty of this moment, nearly divine. *This is what life is. This.*

Hold this. Hold it close. Before it's lost to the tides.

For a moment, one single moment, everything stays impossibly still.

Acknowledgements

Making a novel is a team sport, and my eternal gratitude goes to the team who has made Still Me: Jamis, Sharon, and Melissa at Turnstone Press, my amazing editor Kimmy Beach, and my beta readers and sounding boards, who are too numerous to list here. I have been difficult, I have been particular, and I have been obsessed, but it was all for the sake of trying to elevate this book as much as you've all elevated it for me.

My thanks to all those who inspired a little story element here, a character trait there, and a golf moment or two that I could pour in to this story. I would especially like to thank Thomas McBroom for his time, and his openness to allowing his designs to be a key feature in the book!

For what it's worth, I was not raised on golf and I'm not a very good golfer. But I love the game. Bad golf is better than no golf. I hope this book gives you some insight into the most profound elements of the game and inspires you to head out to the course to see if they unveil themselves to you.

And for those who are grieving (and I think many of us are, in these times of COVID-19), know that you are not alone. Death is truly a part of life. May we all find ways to appreciate what is here, now. If you are troubled, talk to someone. They want to listen.

Thank you to all of my family for listening.